FIRE OF JUSTICE

FIRE OF JUSTICE

HAWTHORN ACADEMY BOOK THREE

D.R. PERRY

DISRUPTIVE IMAGINATION®

LMBPN Publishing
PMB 196, 2540 South Maryland Pkwy
Las Vegas, NV 89109

Version 1.00, July 2021
(Previously published as a part of the megabook *Hawthorn Academy: Year One*)
ebook ISBN: 978-1-64971-864-8
Print ISBN: 978-1-64971-865-5

CHAPTER ONE

After Halloween, everyone on campus talked about the incident at the Night Creatures concert. Almost every student had been on the Common that night, but nobody publicly speculated about who the magus behind the mask was. In private, things were different.

"I can't believe nobody agrees with me, that Charity must have done the attack." Faith crossed her arms over her chest, sticking her nose in the air. "Everyone knows my sister's the wicked bitch of Park Avenue."

"Whoa, take it easy there." Dylan stepped back. He didn't like confrontation much, I'd come to realize. "I mean, we believe you. We're your friends, and you know her better than anyone here. But if nobody saw anything, what can they do?"

"Well, they must think somebody here did it." Grace shrugged. "Nobody whispers this much all over campus if they don't suspect someone here."

"I'm totally sure it was Charity." Faith stomped her foot. "I have no proof, but I'm not alone. All her lackeys are walking on eggshells. They must think she did it but can't figure out why they're not in the headmaster's office right now."

"Maybe they're too scared. Or they agree with her." Hal sighed. "But I don't want to believe that."

"What if she's saying it's someone else?" I couldn't stand it anymore, so I walked up to the elephant in the room and punched it right in its lousy trunk. "What if they suspect it's me?"

"Why would anyone think that?" Logan blinked. "You're not popular, but everyone knows you're a good person."

"Everyone does not." Faith sighed. "I know how public opinion works, and people in the upper classes are not cool with Aliyah. No offense, but most students still judge you for the cafeteria and think you set the fire in the lab. Charity's made a scapegoat out of you."

"I think Faith's right." Hal nodded. "The blame game jives with what I read in Charity's file. That masked magus attacked with a fire weapon, one that was hard to put out, like the lab. The attacker wore a mask and made that hill so people couldn't judge their height, and the hill cut us off from the crowd, so nobody saw our friends put the fire out except the band. So yeah, maybe she's blaming Aliyah."

"We're doing something about it, then." Grace set her jaw. "She can't go around spreading rumors about one of the people who stopped the fire. That's just wrong."

"You're right." Faith nodded. "But when I went to Headmaster Hawkins on Halloween, he just took a statement. It wasn't enough, my word alone against whatever she might have said."

"Maybe more of us need to go to him and make our own statements." Logan stood up. "It can't hurt."

Logan totally made sense, so that was what we did. All five of my friends from school went in separately to see the headmaster, even though they all had less proof than Faith. We had extra time now that nobody did Familiar Bonding anymore.

Tuesday went by, and Wednesday. Charity didn't get in trouble, but neither did I. My friends all saw me putting out the fire, which meant Charity's blame game couldn't go any farther than the rumor mill.

That night at dinner, there was a series of posters on the walls, announcing an informal party in the lounge for Saturday. It was even fire-themed, something about a hearthside gathering. Charity was throwing it.

She's trying another way to get you on probation. Or worse, expelled.

The evil inside voice had a point, so I decided to make myself scarce over the weekend. I told my roommate about it as I packed a knapsack before bed, but Grace didn't like that idea at all.

"Aliyah, you shouldn't leave. You're letting her win if you do." Grace paced the room, swinging her bathroom bag in one hand. "You should just go to her party and say it's stupid, then go to the library or something."

"But who knows what she'll try to pin on me if I stick around?" I leaned against the wall on the side of my bed. "If I'm not even on campus, all that happens is she threw a party I missed." I dropped my roommate a wink. "So, I'm going home."

"I guess you have a point." Grace sighed. "If that's your plan, don't stay too late."

"I guess I can go early in the morning before breakfast." I patted Ember, who was asleep in my lap. "That ought to do it."

"Well, you'd better inform the headmaster then, so the doors will be open. They're locked after lights out until breakfast time." She turned her back, finally heading to the restroom for her bedtime routine.

"Hey, Grace." She stopped. "Thanks for believing in me."

"You'd do the same." She waved and headed out the door.

I took my roommate's advice, sending a message to the head-master before setting an alarm so I could leave at the crack of dawn on Saturday, but I had to make it through Thursday and Friday first—and Friday was sort of a big deal. It was a Bishop's Row game but also a tryout.

"Listen up because I'm only telling you maggots once." Coach Pickman paced in front of the bleachers, where we all sat during Thursday's Gym period. "This game is important because this is how we pick your year's team. You know, the one that's going up against all the upperclassmen this spring?"

"That's not fair." Bailey snorted. "Second and third years have always gotten two teams each, and we only get one."

"If you want to talk to me about always, don't complain." Coach Pickman laughed *at* us, not *with* us. "If we keep things the way they've always been, you won't compete at all. Shut your yaps and be thankful. And play your hearts out."

Our time in Gym that day was spent on drills: conjuring, throwing, and ducking each other's balls. Hal didn't use any of his special moves, and I didn't blame him. He'd want to save his stamina for the game. He'd told us all about a million times how he much wanted to be on the team.

In the library, I even found him looking over books of game strategies with Faith. She gave him advice instead of taking notes, which made me think she'd given up on making the team to help her boyfriend. She had changed an awful lot in a good way.

At dinner, none of us could eat. Our to-go bags sat half full. When we went upstairs for the night, we all brought leftovers. I fed mine to Ember.

On the way downstairs in the morning, we wished each other luck. Soon enough, Logan, Faith, Hal, and I were in the gym, waiting to get started.

We'd figured out our formation earlier in the week. Since Hal was so good at dodging, he was up front, on first. Unlike in many other sports, it was a defensive position. I was fast, so I was on second defense. Logan was right behind me—second mid was what they called that. He was slow and his water magic matched, but that was a good thing.

If I ducked, Logan might still be holding his ball. One way to avoid getting tagged out was bumping the incoming ball with yours, but that only worked if you hadn't launched it yet. The lag in Logan's magic meant he'd most likely manage that tactic.

Bailey was beside him on first mid. That was mostly because we weren't concerned if she got tagged out. Her air magic wasn't much use against the other side, in large part because both her sister and Dylan were air and more likely to make the first-year team. The other drawback to her magic was that it couldn't move most of the other elements. It only affected fire, and Kitty wasn't likely to be much of a threat.

Alex was in the back, playing reverse point. That was what we called the position between the columns. Reverse point was the most balanced player, the one whose magic and athleticism were about even. Normally, that would have been me, but I couldn't risk revealing myself as an extramagus to get on an intramural team, hence Alex's promotion. I shouldn't have minded, but I did.

I'd had a long conversation on Monday with Logan about how I should be reverse point, because technically I was the strongest player. But without the ability to fully unleash my magic, I couldn't play to my potential. I had to minimize just about every move I made on the court, and that stung. The very fact that he understood had softened that blow

Our familiars acted sort of like a cheering squad. They hung around on the sidelines, watching us. Most of them were openly excited, except for Alex's basilisk Aceso, who curled up in a scaly ball with her head on her tail. I was exhausted too, so I didn't blame her.

Coach Chen watched over the coin toss. Eston called heads, leaving us with tails, but we won, so Hal returned victorious. That meant we got the first throw. I conjured my fire, forming it into a ball between my hands. It was practically second nature at that point, but the flames crackled in response to the nervous excitement singing through my veins.

Coach Pickman blew the whistle and I threw, aiming directly for Dylan. It was a long shot because he played reverse point, but if I tagged him out, we'd win the game immediately.

Everyone said he was the strongest player in our year, but I had at least as good a throwing arm as he did. Also, somewhere deep down, I wanted to impress him.

But he was prepared, or at least his team was. My throw would hit him since I'd aimed properly and he had no time to dodge, but Kitty leaped out from her position behind Grace, taking a hit that immediately removed her from play. Her ankyr and cestus absorbed the magic, flashing red to indicate she was out. She jogged back to the bleachers while everybody else had their orbs halfway conjured or more. I noticed Lee was especially fast at this. I'd have to watch out for him as well as Dylan.

I had got another fireball ready before Lee's wooden orb reached me. I hung onto my ball, incinerating his because fire almost always beat wood. After that, I dodged left as Eston's water projectile buzzed past me. It was always better to go toward the middle of the court than risk eliminating yourself by stepping over the line on the right.

Logan was there, his orb absorbing Eston's. When two types of magic hit each other, the outcome varied depending on the elements. Water added to water, so Logan had no choice. He needed to throw his too-heavy orb or banish it and conjure another.

He tossed underhand, aiming at Grace, who played first defense opposite me. She dropped to the floor, flat on her face, the orb of umbral magic held over her head. It was an amazing dodge, brilliant even, because she skipped up off the floor almost right away afterward. That move right there would probably get her on the first-year team.

I was on one knee, but if I didn't launch my fireball soon, it'd be too hot to handle. I aimed for Hailey, knowing that air fed fire. She'd dodged in front of Dylan to avoid her own sister's airball, so it was possible I might get a two-in-one throw.

The fireball hit Hailey straight on. Since she had her ball over her head, preparing to throw it, my magic hit her ankyr, which flashed red. She stomped off toward the bleachers, glaring over her shoulder at Bailey, who'd somehow managed to last longer than her despite being less powerful.

"We're getting killed out here. Come on, guys!" Dylan clapped his hands. It was only then that I realized he'd launched his ball.

"Asshole!" Bailey jumped in front of Alex, taking the hit in a move similar to Kitty's.

"Language." Coach Pickman blew her whistle." If you weren't out, you would be now."

Hal sidestepped, avoiding Grace's umbral magic. In the space he'd previously occupied, Alex made his throw. The poison magic headed directly toward Dylan, who hadn't finished conjuring his next water ball yet. Grace couldn't defend him either, but Lee came to his rescue.

The wood Magus threw a brown spiky ball in an atypical play. Instead of jumping up to block the poison while holding his projectile, he tried to bump it out in midair.

Lee had amazing aim, but his throwing power left something to be desired. He didn't manage to deflect the poison all the way out of bounds. Instead of vanishing after crossing the line, the poison ball hit Eston. Lee did too, but in Bishop's Row, the ankyr and cestus are programmed to account for friendly fire without penalty.

His ankyr flashed red, and he left the court to sit next to Kitty. Faith took some initiative at that point. She'd been holding her undeath magic back all this time, in no small part because it was more dangerous than most other elements in Bishop's Row. Practically nothing but fire could beat it. And, like with poison, any player whose ankyr weren't on exactly right could end up in the infirmary if it hit them.

Faith threw at Grace. Dylan was too far away to protect her. Then again, that wasn't his job. She was the one playing defense, and you couldn't fault Faith for trying to make what was probably her only throw count.

Grace only just managed to conjure a ball of umbral magic to block the incoming orb, which dissipated on impact. Normally this would just mean that Grace had to keep conjuring, but because Faith had held back for so long, her projectile was twice the strength of my roommate's.

Not only did that undeath orb destroy Grace's next one, it bled through and hit her ankyr. They flashed red, and she was out—in more ways than one.

She hit the court, falling on her side, thank goodness. Lee followed up by tossing a wood orb at Faith in retaliation, striking her out, but I could see it was worth the risk.

Faith's play had totally intended consequences. She'd used strategy from the library books, which included getting in the other players' heads. With his girlfriend down, Dylan froze, a big mistake while playing this sport.

Alex struck. He wasn't quite as fast as me with creating his orbs. That meant his projectile wasn't as strong as mine. Dylan's air orb would block Alex's poison, but there was no way he could dodge two at the same time while he stared slack-jawed at Grace on the floor.

I left myself open to Lee's next attack, pitching on a curve. It was a long shot, but either I'd hit Dylan or Hal would. He was still in play somewhere on the court.

My fireball blazed by, narrowly missing Dylan's head as he tilted his neck to one side. Maybe it was even accidental, but that was okay.

Hal's space magic came in like a wrecking ball. He'd been conjuring since Grace's last throw, so the orb he tossed was too big to dodge. Dylan gave it a try, tensing his legs to jump over it, but he didn't leap in time.

His ankyr flashed red, and he was out. Game over.

Coach Pickman blew her whistle while Coach Chen took more notes. We were all a bit out of sorts, but otherwise okay. Even Grace sat up, not any the worse for wear after getting hit by that undeath orb.

But Hal was breathless and pale, like the day he'd ended up in the infirmary. Faith rushed away from the bleachers and to his side. Dylan crossed the court's midline. Between the two of them, they got Hal to a seat. Nin immediately bounced into his lap. Seth tried to pull the cooler over, but he was too small. Ember, Doris, and Gale helped him by pushing from the back.

"Overtaxed, huh?" Coach Pickman strode over to Hal. "Nice strategy out there, Hawkins, but you'd better build some stamina before next semester if you want us to win anything."

"What?" Hal held an ice-cold bottle against his forehead.

"You're on the first-year team."

"How?"

"The other years don't even have a space magus. They can't counter any of the plays we can do with you on defense. As long as you didn't choke out there today, including you was always our plan."

"What about the rest?"

"Chen's on that now. You'll find out after your Turkey Day break. Take a rest. Dubois, you too. Full-force undeath orbs are no joke." She turned her back to walk away but added, "Not bad, Fairbanks. Not bad."

"Who, me?" Faith blinked.

Coach Pickman either didn't hear her or pretended not to. It didn't much matter. Faith went totally silent, face pale, eyes wide, until Hal took her hand, and she blushed. She pulled him closer, tilting his head so it rested on her shoulder.

Watching them, you'd never have thought she was the second meanest girl on campus just ten weeks ago. I'd almost fought her, which would have begun a cycle of harm and retaliation that might never have ended. Hal stopped that, just by caring. It was no surprise to me. Love was important; I'd had ample demonstration of that in my family. But I'd never understood how much of a difference it could make for people who'd gone through life with the bare minimum.

Some of what you learned in school had nothing to do with class-rooms and everything to do with the people you met there.

I woke and dressed in darkness the next morning, escorted through the doors by the headmaster because avoiding an attack isn't just a strategy for Bishop's Row. Refusing to attend one party was no big deal if it'd keep my friends and me out of trouble. On the way down Essex Street, I thought that lesson about caring from yesterday was over.

But it had only just begun.

Thanksgiving was just another weekend at home for me, but for Dylan, Grace, and Lee, it'd be time spent on campus alone. Because my roommate was Canadian, her version of the holiday was already past. The bus back to her aunt's wasn't too expensive, but she'd told me there was little point. Nobody in the UK or mainland China observed the day, either.

Hal and his family usually had dinner in the cafeteria on campus together, but this year, they'd be missing Hal's grandpa and mom.

Even with the three students from abroad in attendance with them, it would be lonely.

The last thing I wanted on my mind all weekend was my friends and the headmaster rattling around on campus like the last handful of peas in a can, which was why I asked my parents if we had room for five more.

My folks said yes, so I invited everybody. Grace and Dylan accepted just about right away. Lee hesitated but decided to go once he found out Izzy and Cadence always came over to hang out after dinner. They all asked about spending time around town, but everything was closed on Thanksgiving day besides the hospital and gas stations.

Hal knew all this, of course. Technically, he was a Salem local too. He definitely wanted to come but had to ask his father. He talked to me about it the next day in the library.

"I'll attend, Aliyah. Dad won't, though."

"What's up?"

"He's not saying." Hal shook his head. "But this is pretty typical for him. My dad doesn't much like going into Salem. Not since last year, anyway."

"Well, okay. As long as he knows he's welcome."

"Oh, yeah, he definitely does. It's nothing personal."

"I'm kinda surprised you're coming, Hal." Logan shrugged. "I mean, I'd have figured you'd take the train down to New York with Faith."

"Oh, I wasn't invited." Hal sighed.

"Are you okay?" Logan blinked.

"Yeah. It's her parents. They never invite guests on Thanksgiving, only family."

"Should have figured. Sorry." Logan winced. "Guess they're a bit like my folks that way. I'm dreading going home."

"By the way, what are you going to do about Doris?"

"I already asked to board her with your grandma, Aliyah." Logan grinned. "My parents had a devil of a time trying to get Gale on the plane when they sent him here with me, so they just think I'm doing things the easy way. They paid the fees, too."

"They're going to find out eventually." Faith paused on her way past our table with a book. "You can't hide something as personal as a familiar from anyone for long."

"Good thing they live in Vegas, then." Logan leaned back, letting Doris leap into his lap. "It'll take them way longer to figure it out."

"Still." She sighed. "They'll pitch a major fit, and it's gonna hurt. Are you sure you want that at some unknown point in the future instead of at a time you've picked?"

"Faith's got a good point." I nodded. "We should plan it out." Doris purred. "See? She likes that idea."

But Logan either didn't agree, or he was just not ready to think about it. At least there was time, but not before this holiday.

CHAPTER TWO

We had no classes on Wednesday, although the cafeteria was open so students could still have meals before heading for the airport or train stations. Logan had departed the night before on a red-eye flight, leaving Doris with Ember and me. I'd bring her to Bubbe's tonight when I went home.

In the early morning, the campus felt almost normal, but the rest of the day was an exercise in reduction. Dylan, Grace, Lee, and I waited through the day together, watching our classmates leave campus.

Hal spent every moment he could with Faith, who was pale and fidgety. Seth was nervous, too, despite Nin's and Ember's best efforts to cheer him up. He had that same snippy energy as the day I'd met him in Bubbe's office, which finally made sense.

Faith's abrasive attitude must have been defensive, designed to protect her from a toxic and apparently large family. Izzy had mentioned to me last weekend that there was a psychic Fairbanks boy at Messing who was a year ahead of her, with another to follow in the next. Apparently, the younger one was the twin of Faith's little sister, Temperance. The boy at Izzy's school acted like the dudebro version of Charity. A bully. Ugh.

After dinner, we left campus together. It was time for Faith to catch her train, which she had booked separately from her sister. I'd asked if she felt safe traveling alone. She'd said Charity was the most dangerous person she could think of. We all insisted on seeing her off.

It was cold enough that we could see our breath. Ember and Gale got a kick out of that happening to people. Their amusement reminded me of being a kid and the games I'd play with Noah outside in winter, pretending to be dragon shifters. I held Doris part of the way, but eventually she got down. Mercats can tolerate lower temperatures with ease.

Nin rode with Seth in his tote. Hal and Faith held hands the entire way down Essex and then Washington Street. Scratch stayed tucked under Lee's overcoat instead of walking on the ice-rimed cobblestones, peeking out at times to chirp at Doris and Lune. The moon hare must have been used to colder weather than this because he hopped along like it was no big deal.

At the train station, we said goodbye, the rest of us turning to give Hal and Faith some privacy. Dylan took Grace's hand, squeezing. She squeezed back. Gale swooped overhead, chasing Ember in circles around the parking lot's streetlamps. Lune just leaned his head against Grace's foot, a common display of affection between them.

We waited until the train pulled away, waving at Faith. She'd have to switch to an Amtrak in Boston, but the Commuter Rail out of Salem only took half an hour. She could go right to bed when she got home, avoiding her siblings for that much longer. She warned us that she might be extra cranky when she returned on Sunday.

After that, we all walked back to campus. The rest of my friends would stay in the dorms until dinner tomorrow, but I went home, thank goodness. Noah had already left at lunchtime, so he'd probably been baking and helping set up tables for hours.

We waved goodbye at the school door, which was next to one of the bank's barred windows that night. After that, I walked down Essex Street with Ember on my shoulder and Doris by my side. The street was almost deserted. The only person out was Azreal. He didn't have his cart at that hour so he trotted to catch up with me, chatting good-naturedly about how Gallows Hill was having its first Bishop's Row tournament this year.

"But how?" I blinked. "You sort of need to conjure magic to play it."

"Plenty of changelings have magic, and even the ones who don't can always conjure glamour away from their appearance." Az chuckled. "It's going to make us look extra scary on the court, too. Want to see?"

"Some other time, Az." I grinned. "Probably not a good idea out here in the street. But that's cool. We find out who's on our team this year after we get back from break."

"Wait." He gasped. "They're letting first years play?"

"Yeah." I shrugged, jostling a peep from Ember. "I'm not sure why. They've never done it that way before, but I'm glad since I like playing."

"To me, it feels like at Gallows Hill, we're practicing for something." He scratched his head. "We've got as many teams as you guys do at Hawthorn, but I don't know what they're planning, so keep your eyes and ears open on campus after break. I'll do the same, and we can compare notes another time."

"Sounds like a plan." We were at the corner of Hawthorne Street, so we said goodbye and I turned toward my house. "Thanks for walking with me."

"Hey, what are friends for?" He waved and turned back down Essex Street.

I'd never considered Azreal a close friend, but he'd looked out for the other townie kids for years. Goblin changelings can scare pretty much anyone when they drop their glamour, and he'd always used that power to chase off bullies and the crueler sorts of tourists.

I know Izzy wasn't interested in romance, but someday, I hoped he'd find a partner in crime. He always seemed lonely, despite his many siblings. I suppose being the only changeling in the family was similar to being an only child.

I stopped at Bubbe's office, where she was expecting me. Doris padded across the threshold and down the hall. I followed, watching as she curled up on a cushion near the kitchen sink. Bubbe left a basin of water in there in case she had to take a dip at some point. I gave my grandma a hug before heading up the back stairs.

At home, there wasn't much for me to do except clean. Everything we cooked the night before was already done, cooling on racks or stowed in the fridge, so I washed dishes, pots, pans, and utensils. I also rinsed the serving platters and bowls we only used for big meals.

When I was done, my arms were tired, my eyelids heavy, and my hands pruned and itchy from all the soap and water. Ember peeped from her perch on top of the refrigerator, where she'd surely been sneaking biscuits, judging by the roundness of her belly.

"Yeah, girl, okay. It's time for bed." I headed toward the stairs, and when I got there, I practically crawled up them. I was just that tired. I managed to put my pajamas on, though. I didn't want to sleep in my leggings and tunic, even though they were pretty comfortable. Nothing beat flannel for bedtime during Salem's brisk autumn weather.

I hadn't brought any clothes home from school, so there was no laundry to do. I'd just wear what I had at home all weekend. We didn't do much besides hang out around the house and go for walks around town as a family the day after Thanksgiving. I could include my friends from school in all that stuff if they wanted.

As I brushed my teeth, I found myself wondering why Noah had never invited anybody home, not last year or this one either. There were plenty of other students who lived halfway around the world from Hawthorn Academy. Maybe not as far away as Lee from China, but at least one of the kids in Noah's year came from Costa Rica, and there was a third-year from Poland.

It crossed my mind, what Bubbe said about the difference between my brother and me. How he was always afraid, and how I didn't stop and think. It was almost like we were opposites. Noah had been at the Parents' Night dance alone, which meant he didn't have a date. I wonder if he got turned down, or if he just didn't bother asking anyone from fear of rejection.

Was Darren the one who'd asked him out, or was it the other way around?

I practically leaped out of my skin because somebody spoke. I managed to spit into the sink and not on the mirror, thank goodness.

"Oh, he asked me out." Noah stood in the doorway, which meant Ember hadn't spontaneously started speaking English and imitating my brother's voice. "And we're never, ever getting back together. Not ever."

"Okay, Noah. Back away from the protestations." I rinsed my toothbrush, watching the water carry foamy toothpaste down the drain. "Sorry about my wayward inside voice, but it was about due for an outburst."

"It happens." He shrugged.

"So, what's up?" I was relieved we were having a relatively normal conversation.

"Just here to brush my teeth, much like my sister, who's hogging the bathroom."

"I'll be out of your way in a sec." I tapped the toothbrush against the sink to get the water off, put it away, then wash my hands and got out of his way. "Good night, Noah."

"Good night, Aliyah."

I headed into my room, closing the door behind me and treading carefully to avoid bumping my head on the ceiling. I hoped I remembered it was low in the morning so I didn't have to spend all of Thanksgiving Day with a bump on the head. I fell asleep almost as soon as my head hit the pillow.

I didn't get a goose egg. I got dressed and helped my parents. Bubbe came up with the baked goods she'd finished in the downstairs oven. She also let Doris come upstairs to share the holiday with the rest of us, which was good because I didn't want to think of her all alone for the day. After that, it was time for the walk down to Essex Street to meet my friends, but they were already at the intersection with Hawthorne Street. Dylan, Hal, and Grace knew the way. They'd all been here before.

It was time for dinner.

In Salem and most of the rest of New England, that meant it was one in the afternoon. Some people around here had it as early as noon. Why did we have Thanksgiving dinner that early? Because why shouldn't we eat all day instead of having a tiny lunch and then feasting? This was just the way it was done here.

I was well aware that in other parts of the country, folks didn't bring out the turkey until actual dinner time, like five, six, or seven o'clock. An internet friend from Florida had told me they did it even later, like eight, which boggled my mind. Who wanted to wait that long for the main event? I certainly didn't. Even if I moved away from New England, I'd still be cooking turkey on the last Thursday of November so it was done in time for lunch, even though it's dinner. And it'd still be kosher.

"What's up with all the separate plates?" Grace asked.

"It's kosher, right, Aliyah?" Hal tilted his head.

"Right." I nodded.

"Thought that was all about not eating pork and shrimp." She shrugged.

"No, they also don't mix the meat with the milk." Dylan pointed at a cream pie on the dessert table, which was on the other side of the room from the one we had dinner at. "We don't want that on the same plate with turkey, or with the same forks and stuff."

"How did you know?" I blinked.

"Dad's chummy with the guy who runs the kosher deli down the street from our apartment." Dylan chuckled. "I paid attention."

The best way to know whether a dish was successful was by how quiet your guests were during the meal. It was dead silent in there. Nobody talked until they got second helpings. Even our familiars were quiet. They had their own meals of scraps selected by Bubbe.

"What's that?" Asked Lee.

"Cranberry sauce, the jellied kind," I answered.

"It's a travesty." Noah snorted. "Try the homestyle stuff. I made it. And have some sweet potato pancakes with it. Bubbe makes those."

"The turkey is amazing." Hal grinned. "Who made it?"

"My husband, the gourmet chef." Mom smiled. "He grew all the herbs he rubbed on it himself."

"I'm not a gourmet." Dad chuckled, dropping her a wink. "You are. Whose idea was it to make cinnamon corn? That's what I call fancy."

"I like the potatoes best." Grace spooned another helping of them onto her plate. "How do you get them creamy like this without butter or milk?"

"Coconut milk." I got myself a helping of beets and sweet potatoes. "Non-dairy milk is super versatile."

It was hard to believe it, but after getting the dinner plates and utensils in the dishwasher, we all had room for dessert. I helped Noah move the sweet stuff to the table, along with the dairy plates and utensils.

"What's this one?" Lee pointed at the casserole Noah cut into. "Almost looks like a dinner dish."

"Noodle kugel." I laughed. "And of course, he's already attacking it. Noah ate almost an entire pan of that after school let out last spring."

"It's the best comfort food ever. It's got raisins in it." He hefted his full plate. "Who doesn't like raisins?"

"Me." Dylan wrinkled his nose. "What's that bread? Does it have chocolate in it?"

"That's my babka." Bubbe nodded. "Yes, it does. Try some! And the rugelach. It's raspberry." She put some of each on a plate and handed it to him.

I got myself some too, plus small slices of apple and pumpkin pie. Grace got rugelach and apple pie. Lee tried a little of everything, although he went back for more babka.

Every year, I was amazed at how much baking Bubbe managed to do. My grandma made all the cookies, the challah, and that decadent babka in the kitchen downstairs. She made more this year than on any other because we'd never had this many guests.

After everyone rested, we sat watching a rerun of the Macy's Day parade in the living room. Halfway through that, Izzy and Cadence came by to join us. We chatted about the floats, wondering how they used to make them without magic back before the Reveal.

It was almost too cold this year to take a walk outside. We had to, though. My friends from Hawthorn needed to head back eventually.

We needed the exercise too after all that food, so we sat, planning our route to include a pass by the wharf.

Bubbe had care packages for our foray outside, baggies of rugelach and babka slices, with a thermos each full of hot cocoa. For Lee, Dylan, and Grace, she'd also packed up a second dinner and dessert, so they'd have more for later if they wanted it. We headed down the stairs and out of the building together. Noah even came along.

The streets were quiet, nearly deserted, the polar opposite of Halloween the month before. It'd be a bleak and lonely scene without company, so that was one reason to be thankful for my friends and family this year. The world was a magically beautiful place, and company only enhanced it.

CHAPTER THREE

"I can't believe this." Faith blinked, her hand at her chest in a gesture I'd come to recognize as her expression of shock.

"I honestly think nobody can." Bailey turned her nose up in the air, snorting at Faith. "You're just going to make us lose games. I have no idea why they put you on the team, even though you're in reserves."

"How dare you." I planted my feet, placing my hands on my hips and looking Bailey right in the eye. "After the first day of Gym, you barely made any effort. Faith busted her ass, and now you're criticizing her. And you used to call yourself her friend! Don't try to deny it, just shut up and go away."

Bailey stood there, her mouth opening and closing like a goldfish that had accidentally jumped out of the bowl in the face of my anger, which made sense. I practically spontaneously combusted my first day here. I'd since managed to lengthen my fuse, but it was shorter when someone else got attacked.

"Whoa, Aliyah." Logan put his hand on my shoulder, reminding me of the way Noah used to help me chill out. "Tone it back a little, okay?" He gave it one more pat, then broke contact.

I guessed what he was thinking; I might have conjured solar magic in front of everybody, but the verbal outburst had helped me blow off steam and avoid an extramagus accident. It was nice to know my friends cared, though. Logan wasn't the only one supporting Faith or my defense of her.

Grace and Hal flanked me, both staring daggers at Bailey. Behind us, I heard Faith gasp like she'd taken her first breath after swimming several laps underwater. She couldn't possibly be surprised we took her side, so there must have been something else going on.

Sure enough, Coach Pickman strode past Bailey, stepping between us, her presence cutting through the tension like a hot knife through butter. Our anger didn't break as much as dissipate, which was a good thing because even though I had my solar magic under control, fire was another story. It was harder to curb in general.

"Enough." Coach Pickman brandished her whistle in my general direction. "Supporting your teammates is fine." She glanced at Bailey. "Giving your classmates grief is not. Fighting in here is unacceptable. No more of this in my gym, or you're all doing laps for the rest of the year."

Bailey spun on her heel, flouncing away from us. Good thing she did, because Faith couldn't take any more high emotion, not even the positive kind. She dashed toward the girl's locker room, her breath hitching. Seth jumped up from the cozy pile of familiars on the bleachers and followed her, his little paws tapping on the floor.

I turned to go after her, but Grace stopped me.

"Let me. You need to calm down." She turned around and took off across the court, following Faith. "I'll send Lune if we need you." The moon hare hopped after her.

Coach Pickman barked orders at Logan and Bailey, directing them to go get our equipment. Alex sauntered away from the team list, grinning. He had good reason because he was on it, although Dylan was playing Reverse Point. He headed our way and I was about to wave, but there was a tug at my sleeve.

"Shouldn't I go after her too?" Hal asked me. But someone else answered.

"Are you kidding?" Alex put a hand on his shoulder. "You're the headmaster's son, but you're still a boy, and that's the girl's locker room. Besides, you look like you need to sit down."

That was how I ended up sitting on the bleachers with Hal Hawkins, trying to banish this sense of unease instead of celebrating the fact that almost all of our friends had made it onto the team. The only one who didn't was Logan, and he told me before tryouts that he'd prefer cheering us on anyway.

"Are you guys okay?" Alex Onassis sat down between us. Maybe he meant well, but it'd be hard answering when he wasn't in on my secret, so I let Hal speak first.

"I'll be all right." He leaned forward, propping his elbows on his thighs. "I knew I'd make the list because Coach said so at tryouts, but none of us had any idea Faith would get into the reserves. I guess that included Bailey."

"Yeah, I was surprised too." Alex grinned at me. "I didn't think I'd make it on the team either."

"How come?" One of the best ways to avoid talking about yourself was to ask your conversational partner a question. And boy howdy, did I want to avoid talking about magic.

"Lee is just so fast. His wood magic may not let him conjure very powerful orbs at this point, but I figured that would be more valuable on the team than my garden-variety average-speed poison."

"Average is exactly what Bishop's Row needs, though, right?" I shrugged.

"No, you're confusing average with balance." Alex's eyes lit up as he talked about the sport. I guess he was the closest thing we had to a jock. "Which I guess I have, but you've got more power. The best Bishop's Row players have mundane reflexes, balance, and conjuring swiftness, plus magical power, control, and speed in equal measure. By those standards, you're all that and a bag of chips. I always wondered why you didn't volunteer to play reverse point during tryouts in the first place."

"Um." I wasn't sure what to say, but Hal came to my rescue.

"She lacks control sometimes." Hal winced. "Sorry, Aliyah, but surely you remember the first day of school?"

"Oh, yeah, right." Alex directed another question at me. "Is that why it always feels like you're holding back in here? At Gym I mean? The only thing you go all out with athletically is plain old mundane running."

"You could be reserved just like me, Alex." I let snark be my guide. "All you have to do is nearly burn down a cafeteria. Once." I snorted. "And have people blame you for lab fires you didn't set. After that, you're too nervous to cut loose with much of anything, magically speaking."

"I've always wondered about that." He scratched his head. "Did you really get into it with Charity Fairbanks? Weren't you afraid?"

"Definitely." I nodded. "She's a scary person, and Noah told me all about her last year. But it would've been worse to just let her have her way."

I was about to launch into an explanation of how I wasn't the only person who'd ever stood up to Charity—after all, Alex was sitting right next to Hal, who'd done more than his fair share of confronting the mean girl—but Coach Pickman blew her whistle.

Grace went off to her next class, Faith returned from the locker room, and it was time to do all our Gym exercises. Bailey grumbled about practically everything, probably because she was still sour about not making the team. Logan kept on keeping on. He smiled, laughed with Hal, and helped us improve. The easy set of his shoulders told me he wasn't stressed about this, that making the team might have been harder for him in a way. He hated being the center of attention, after all.

I didn't much like it either, but it was nearly impossible to avoid at that point my academic career at Hawthorn Academy. I hoped I could handle myself both on and off the court since it felt like everyone's eyes were on me, even though they'd had two entire months for that before our team assignments.

Alex, in particular, watched me like a hawk. When he wasn't looking, his basilisk was. I wondered why. Maybe he had some strategy in mind for Bishop's Row, but exams took up all of my time, so I didn't get the chance to find out about it until much later.

The exams were all on paper. There were no lab practicals on midterms for the first years. I breathed a sigh of relief as Professor Luciano explained this in homeroom. Exam anxiety was something I went through, and the last thing I wanted was to get involved in another lab incident. I felt like I wasn't ready to be tested on what we'd learned in there anyway. From the looks on my classmates' faces, almost everyone agreed.

Hal was the exception. He'd become quite good at labs because he approached them like a recipe using magical ingredients. All semester, he'd chatted about the things he'd learned to cook before starting here.

Making food had been a huge part of my upbringing, too. I just couldn't get my brain around the magic part because so much of my experience was mundanely based. Maybe if my family had used magical recipes, I'd have been more comfortable in there.

During the tests, our familiars were in the gym, hanging out and playing games with the coaches. That kept them from distracting us and had the added benefit of letting them blow off steam during an extremely stressful time for all of us. I raised my hand.

"Professor, will we be able to see how they're doing in there? I mean, if we finish early or something?"

"You will, in fact." His smile was kinder than I'd ever seen it. If Luciano had a soft spot, it was for critters. "But it won't matter whether you finish early. Coach Chen has agreed to record your familiars as they play. That way, you all get to see what they were up to once your exams are finished. You can even bring the recording home to show your parents if you'd like."

Logan swallowed audibly. I probably only heard it because he sat right behind me, but I knew who wouldn't bring a video home. I wondered how he'd get away with leaving Doris here for almost a month. Mercats needed their magi when they lived on land. When I'd asked him that morning whether he'd board Doris with Bubbe again, he'd said he wasn't sure.

We spent every library session between Thanksgiving and winter break studying for exams. The Ashfords were super helpful with this, having set aside all of the first-year material and putting it in a temporary section just for us. The one drawback was, we couldn't check any books out, but that was understandable. I could only imagine what it might have been like for folks in Charity's year if she'd been able to deprive people she didn't like of the means to study.

At dinnertime, we continued our practice of ordering to-go bags from Penelope and Sandy. Even with the differences in our coursework, it was beneficial for both Luciano's and DeBeer's students to study together. Because of this, Eston and Kitty joined in, along with Lee. Kitty was practically a genius, but Eston needed help with Extrahuman History, and she wanted to get him as many study buddies as possible.

Hal quizzed him on specific stuff, but the rest of us tried giving him a few general study tips. The person who helped most was Logan. He had tons of alternative study hacks. It seemed like water magi had more trouble focusing than most. This was a problem for fire magi, too, but not in the same way. When Logan suggested wearing noise-canceling headphones without any music in them, Eston was amazed to find it a useful strategy.

In the first week of December, Alex started hanging around at dinner without studying, or at least he didn't seem to be. I don't know every learning style, though. Maybe just sitting nearby and listening to us discuss all the material helped him wrap his brain around it. Maybe learning by osmosis wasn't a joke.

Dylan and Logan both sat closer to me while Alex was around. Gale and Doris even came over to hang with Ember during those times. I wasn't sure why, and I didn't bother asking. It might make Logan feel awkward, and as far as Dylan went, I already had a big brother. I really didn't want to start feeling like he was a de facto sibling. The idea just bothered me.

Halfway through the last week of school, I was in the bathroom, brushing my teeth and otherwise getting ready for bed. Faith walked in for what I'd come to recognize as her weekly dip in the baths. She did laps and everything. This time she hung around at the counter, as though waiting for me to finish making my dentist happy with my mad toothbrushing skills.

"Do you like Alex?" She looked me in the eye indirectly, using the mirror as a buffer. I didn't blame her. This was an odd sort of conversation for me to have with anyone, let alone Faith.

"He's okay, I guess. A good athlete." I still couldn't put my finger on what it was about Alex that bothered me, so I repeated what I'd heard from other people. "But he's sort of like Switzerland. Totally neutral about everything, isn't he? Why do you ask?"

"I think he's into you."

"I had no idea." I blinked. "Thought he was just being friendly."

"You seem to notice just about every other social dynamic, Aliyah." She shook her head. "It's not a good idea to ignore stuff like this."

"It's not likely I'll end up with anyone anytime soon." Why was I thinking about Dylan and Grace all of a sudden? "I'm too busy for dating, anyway."

"Well, dating isn't too busy for you, it seems." She snorted. "It's dangerous to just ignore stuff like people having unrequited crushes on you."

"What?" I blinked because this didn't make any sense to me. Dangerous?

"Peep?" Ember swooped down off the counter and peered up at Faith, Seth mimicking her expression almost perfectly. They both looked almost as baffled as I felt. I guess attraction in the critter world was way less complicated.

"I don't know much about Alex. Maybe he's okay. But some people get downright nasty if they feel rejected." Her small smile was surprisingly gentle. "I'm not gonna stand here and tell you I'm worried about you getting hurt. You can take care of yourself in a fight. But subtlety isn't your thing, and there are other ways people harm each other. I'm not trying to be a bitch here, just give you a heads up."

"Thanks, Faith." I nodded. "I'll try talking to Alex alone."

"Maybe find out more about him first. Ask around before you decide." She looked down at the sink. "I did that before making things official with Hal."

"If there's time." I shook my head. "It might be hard finding any."

"Our friends keep watching you. They're worried for you over your thing." She looked up at one of the solar lights and then at my hands. "Exam stress. If you want to talk to Alex and need me to head them off, let me know."

"Thanks." I packed up my bathroom stuff. "Have a good swim, Faith. Thanks for straightening my crown instead of knocking it off."

"You've done that much for me already." She waved. "See you tomorrow."

That conversation had gone better than I ever would've dreamed. Taking advice from Faith Fairbanks was something I would have flat-out laughed at in the first week of school even if Izzy had predicted it, but now she was looking out for me. Who'd have thought?

CHAPTER FOUR

Just when I thought my night would end on a high note, I walked into my room to find Grace on her bed sobbing. Ember swooped down, landing on her headboard. I brought a box of tissues and sat at the foot of her bed, reaching out to take her hand. She let me, only just barely squeezing back. Lune lay beside her, lifting his head briefly to acknowledge my presence. He pressed his chin against her shoulder, keeping it there even as it shook with sobs.

I didn't say anything, just sat there. It had to be rough on her, the prospect of holiday break. The postcard on the bed beside her spoke volumes with only a sentence. Her aunt had written *Stay at school*. Grace didn't have much to celebrate from the little she'd mentioned of life back in Quebec, and she couldn't even go there. In situations like that, when the people around you seemed to have everything you didn't, words didn't always help.

I sat with her for maybe half an hour before she finally calmed down enough to sit up. Her pillowcase was totally soaked. Probably the pillow under it was too, and she only had one of those, school-issued. Everyone else had brought extras, their favorite and most comforting pillows, throws, and blankets from home. Even Logan, whose parents were neglectful at best. And Faith, who dealt with daily abuse back in New York.

Grace had brought nothing but her familiar and a wardrobe of threadbare clothes. Did her life lack that much comfort, or had she brought so little because she worried it was too shabby for prep school? She never said a word about it or did anything to direct attention to the things she lacked.

I'd noticed it, and had done almost nothing all semester besides lending her a dress. Had I stopped caring? Why? How?

You're an extramagus, that's why. Destined to stop caring about everyone else.

I decided to subvert the inside voice with kindness.

As Grace reached for the box of tissues to blow her nose and dry her eyes, I went to my bed and picked up an extra pillow, then opened the dresser to get a spare pillowcase. I changed the one I'd been using for the clean one, then swapped it with the tear-stained pillow, which I set at the foot of Grace's bed. A small gesture, but better that than nothing.

Grace didn't glance behind her, oblivious to my actions. She wasn't thanking me. That didn't matter. Given the state she was in, manners weren't important. Not everyone who needed help was in a position to be polite, but that didn't somehow make them unworthy.

She picked up her bathroom bag and a change of pajamas. If it weren't for the fact that Faith was having her weekly swim, I'd have worried about leaving her alone in there. She looked out for me, and she'd do the same for Grace. We'd all become friends somehow, despite our extremely different backgrounds.

Lune went after her, turning his head to look up at me before hopping out the door. His ears were up, nose twitching. He cared, too.

Since Grace typically showered at night, I had time, so I got out my contraband communication orb for the first time in two weeks. We hadn't planned on communicating tonight, so I hoped that at least one of my friends from town answered.

After a moment, Cadence's voice greeted me.

"Aliyah, what's up? I thought you'd be studying for exams."

"I was, but there's a problem." I closed my eyes, feeling the sting of threatening tears.

"Not another fire? Or—oh, no." She leaned in, whispering. "You didn't go solar, did you?"

"No, nothing like that." I shook my head. "It's not me. It's Grace, my roommate."

"Oh, no!" Cadence gasped. "Is she okay? Did she get hurt playing Bishop's Row or something?"

"I wish." I told Cadence that Grace's aunt wasn't letting her come home, then I described the scene I'd found in my room tonight.

"Why not invite her to stay with you over the break?" Cadence asked. Her solution to practically everything was adding more people. "I mean, I know your parents would probably have room for her to stay for that amount of time."

"That's a good idea, but I wonder whether she'll take me up on it? Grace has a lot of pride, which is great for some stuff but not so much in this situation."

"Do you think it will hurt to ask?" She chuckled. "Something like that happened at Gallows Hill and asking made all the difference, even though the offer got turned down. Sometimes people just want to feel welcome."

"Yeah, you're right." I nodded. "Thanks, Cadence. I have to go. Somebody's coming."

"Okay, talk to you later."

The orb went dark, which was a good thing because I heard voices in the hall. It wasn't the door opening yet, thank goodness. I wasn't sure who was out there.

Regardless of the mysterious talker's identity, it was time to stow the orb back in my suitcase, zip it up, and tuck it under my bed. Once that was done, I trotted to the door and put my ear against it.

"Mark this one. One of these girls is staying." It wasn't a voice I recognized, but low pitched and probably male.

"Okay. Anybody else on this floor?" The second voice was raspy and slightly higher pitched.

"The kid from the UK. We're already keeping the Hawkins brat's room open, so it doesn't matter whether his roommate is staying here or in China. We'll keep the lights on in there at any rate."

I blinked, wondering who at the school would dare refer to Hal Hawkins as a brat. He was the furthest thing from that, first of all. Second of all, talking like that about a space magus' son in a pocket realm he maintained was sort of a bad idea.

"I know the boss wouldn't be happy if he heard that, so why did you say it?" The second voice asked my unspoken question.

"He knows how some of us feel. Kid takes too much after his mother, and nobody trusts that bitch except the people in her school of misfits. Be glad you don't have to work there. Place gives me the creeps. Named after executions and all."

He was talking about Gallows Hill. So, Hal's mother worked there in some capacity or other, since she was definitely too old to attend as a student. I knew next to nothing about her, just that she and Head-master Hawkins were divorced, and what Cadence had said about a vampire from Rhode Island. The only one who knew more was Hal, and he didn't talk about her.

Hal Hawkins seemed stressed and tired. He'd been peaky and list-less lately, and hadn't been to the infirmary. It worried me, but he wasn't alone. Logan was just as stressed. He'd ripped his cuticles more times than I could count in the last week, so we'd been trying to take it easy as a group. I hoped we'd all get some relief after exams, but my gut told me that was unlikely. The same part of my intuition that said Grace was in serious trouble emotionally.

I wished we could figure all this out. Just sit down and talk, be teenagers. But when you were magical, the world expected more from you. More restrictions, more requirements. Our powers weren't even all that big yet, but our responsibilities were enormous. It was impos-sible to just live life as an extrahuman unless you planned to try going without powers. Or maybe lived on an island in the middle of the ocean.

When Grace returned, I took Cadence's advice and invited her to stay with us. She said she was too tired, she'd think about it later, and we'd talk sometime this week.

But Thursday and Friday went by. I stayed in school all weekend studying, and still Grace kept silent on the matter. She practically clung to Dylan, who was there for her. But she was silent every time I saw her, no matter what company she kept.

I cornered Faith in the bathroom on Sunday morning and point-blank asked her if Grace had talked to her.

"Just a bit, on Wednesday after my swim." She sighed. "It was pretty obvious she'd been crying that night, but she wouldn't say a word about what was wrong. Didn't she tell you?"

"No. I don't even think she's talked to Dylan." I took a deep breath. "This is bad, Faith. I don't know what to do."

"I'll get Hal on it. He's got a way with this sort of thing."

I saw Hal manage to approach Grace exactly once. She avoided him for the rest of the day unless she already had someone with her. That wasn't normal for her, and it wasn't even within the realm of academic stress. That initial hunch about her family might have had merit, then.

I tried putting myself in her shoes. Tried to imagine what it would be like if my parents were dead and gone was nearly impossible, not because I had no imagination at all, and not because I lacked empathy. Maybe it was too enormous to contemplate. I tried thinking about what it would be like to lose Noah instead.

Tears sprang to my eyes. Even though we weren't on the best terms this year, I couldn't handle that. I wasn't sure when Grace became an orphan, only that it must have happened before she came to school. My intuition told me it was years ago, but recently enough that she remembered her parents and how different her life was with them in it.

See where kindness gets you? Closer to your inevitable insanity.

This time, I silenced the voice with action. Doing nothing wasn't an option anymore.

Grace was in crisis, in a medical emergency. Emotional states weren't considered medical by some, but they called it mental health for a reason. So, I went to Nurse Smith on Sunday night before exams.

"So, you're telling me your roommate has been crying, avoiding people she normally hangs out with, and won't talk about it? And it's been going on for how long?"

Nurse Smith had his notepad and vial of magical water out again. Of course. As annoying as it was, I couldn't blame him. He was probably used to students lying about all kinds of things to do with their health that would interfere with their medical care, and it was his job to make sure we were healthy enough to be in school.

"Since Wednesday."

"I see." He jotted something down. "Why are you coming to me now?"

"I went to the rest of our friends, trying to help her together. She just kept brushing us off, though. You're her last hope."

"Students are always under extra stress during exam time, and when that coincides with holidays, it only gets worse. I've seen stuff like this before. I think I can help her, but let's lay off until after the exams. I'll be keeping an eye on her from a distance, but if you see anything you think I need to know, find me immediately."

"What are you going to do?"

"She's staying on campus over the break, so I'll help her then. We'll have privacy and time with no class or sports obligations. As far as what we'll do, that's confidential. But Miss Morgenstern, thank you for coming to me. You don't know how much I appreciate this."

I wasn't sure what to say to that, so I nodded and left. I couldn't find it in myself to smile, not with the situation as grave as it was. But I was somewhat relieved.

The day of exams came. Like so many other rites of passage, the reality of taking the test felt like a tipping point. Let me explain this better.

Gallows Hill was the name of Cadence's school, but also an actual hill in Salem. Back when we were kids in pigtails, all the children in town would sled down it. There was a drop-off at the top, where the sled hung for a heart-stopping moment before tilting to hurtle down. Sitting in the room with the pencil, the blue book, and the Scantron sheet was like that suspended moment.

The rest was a wild ride, full of graphite stains on my hands, paper cuts, and gasping in disbelief as I realized I knew more than I thought I did. When I walked out of the room and down the hall toward the gym to reunite with Ember, I thought maybe I had done better than the C- I expected.

I sat in the gym, cuddling my dragonet and waiting for my classmates to come through the door as they finished. Alex was the first to enter after me, his basilisk Aceso rearing her head up and flicking her tongue out as she glided across the polished wood toward him.

He sauntered over once she had twined up his arm and took a seat beside me. I tried to remember what Faith had said that night in the bathroom and realized I hadn't asked around about Alex. So much had been on my mind since then, beyond the brain fry that came with cramming and spilling all that information back out onto the page afterward.

As it turned out, I needn't have worried. Alex just stayed nearby, letting Ember and Aceso play. I got the impression that he was okay with just being there and not saying a word. Whether that came from being bonded to a reptilian familiar was beyond me. Dragonets were warm-blooded like birds.

I hadn't paid attention to him all semester, not outside of Gym, anyway, so maybe that was typical for Alex. He might be one of those folks who liked quiet companionship or simple things. It seemed odd for a jock, but then again, I was odd for a magus. Who was I to judge?

When the rest of the first years entered the gym, they did it as a group. I caught Faith looking in my direction, her eyes narrowing. Maybe she was trying to figure out if I'd had my chat with Alex. She didn't approach to ask. Hal wasn't looking great, so Faith stayed with him.

Logan made a beeline toward his familiar, oblivious to everything and everyone else. That was how he was after any test, and this exam had been three times as long as any other. It looked like Logan was going into extreme introvert mode, only comfortable interacting with Doris. He didn't ask about boarding her, even when I moved down the bleachers. He noticed me there but only waved without smiling. It seemed he was bringing her to Las Vegas after all.

Once we were released from the academic wing, it was time to go home. My bags were already packed and downstairs in the lobby, waiting. The semester was over, finally. Grace had never told me she wasn't staying with me, but that conversation with Nurse Smith meant she'd be well taken care of on campus. I'd have a little peace at home with my family until January.

Maybe I'd earned that much.

CHAPTER FIVE
INTERLUDE

A Christmas Misery
Grace

Oh, yeah, I was miserable. Don't worry, that was only a little south of normal for me. My life in Québec wasn't the greatest, hadn't been since my parents passed away from carbon monoxide poisoning. Even magical folk get done in by the most mundane and stupid accidents, so replace the batteries in your alarms yearly, kids. And don't run kerosene heat without good ventilation. The more you know...

Anyway, I figured I was tired of being my internally melancholy self in the claustrophobic yet hallowed halls of Hawthorn Academy. It always felt weird in there, like there was too much room and not enough all at the same time. Too much light, also.

Since I'd moved in with my aunt on her farm, I'd anticipated and dreaded wide-open spaces at the same time. That might have had something to do with Lune, my moon hare, finding me that same year, after I turned eleven. He didn't much like being out in the open, so the prospect of going to Hawthorn Academy with its wooden campus between worlds had appealed to both of us.

It had lived up to its expectations and then some. The first few weeks were pretty good, despite the fact that my roommate Aliyah Morgenstern nearly burned down the cafeteria and the lab on the first day of class. It felt exciting, though. And it was such a relief, having a friend who wasn't totally normal. It helped that she was uncommonly honest and kind, even though it turned out she was an extramagus. Normal people kind of freaked me out, so Aliyah being weird helped me relax.

I keep getting off the topic, don't I? Which was that dreaded holiday nobody can escape.

Christmas.

I hated it. If you guessed that the reason for this had something to do with my parents' untimely demise, here's some good news. You win. The bad news is you get nothing because everything about me had something to do with being an orphan. How could it not?

There was this idea, especially in extrahuman circles, that losing your parents made you special somehow, but all I wanted was to be just like everyone else. What I wouldn't have given to have my mom back, even if it meant she'd tell me to put on a little makeup and smile more. Or my dad, even if he'd give my boyfriend seven levels of grief just to be sure he treated me decently. But all I had was this hole in my life.

Anyway, Hawthorn Academy went big at Christmas, and I couldn't go home or otherwise escape the halls decked with holly, the faculty and staff getting jolly, or any of that other crap. My aunt's farm wasn't really my home, and I never counted on it feeling that way. Yeah, I know. I sounded awfully grouchy for a Canadian, but we weren't all sunshine and roses, and if you thought so, you're the one with unrealistic expectations.

The only way for me to get out of this mess of red and green and silver and gold and those little blinking lights that annoyed me so much was to get out on the streets of Salem, which was exactly what I did on Christmas Eve about an hour after the sun went down.

Everybody said it'd be dangerous to walk around in the dark alone. It was true, I'd give them that. We all knew what kinds of things went bump in the night because that was part of Hawthorn's curriculum, but everything in this world was dangerous. Even sleeping in your bed on a night like any other, cozy in winter but lacking oxygen-rich air. Life was a terminal disease.

So, I figured I'd take my chances on the street, searching for something beautiful that didn't tear my heart out while looking at it. Don't get me wrong. This little city was decorated for wintry celebration too, but there was something charmingly pagan about it. That made sense since this was the witch city, after all. Yule decorations were like the more reserved cousin of the garish Christmas kind, and that difference helped my state of mind more than I'd expected.

I was on Washington Street, having walked almost all the way to the end where it intersected with Bridge Street. For a moment, I considered getting on the commuter rail and heading down into Boston, but I'd have been stuck in that large, unfamiliar city unless I turned around immediately and came back because no trains would run the next day. There went Christmas, ruining my mood again.

I turned and continued down the other side of Washington Street. This was one of the main drags in the walkable part of Salem, so it had lots of shops and restaurants and other places where it was fun to window shop. That was the only kind of shopping I did because I was poor as dirt. It was good, though, because I got inspirations to make my own things, and there was no shortage of materials in Creatives class.

I flipped the bird at the fake wooden Indian outside the smoke shop. I'm real, and preferred the term "indigenous," thank you very much. Canada was awfully enlightened when it came to things like health care and good citizenship, but it had a long way to go before it did right by us. The United States wasn't much different. I got better treatment here due to being a magus than I would have if I were mundane, though.

On the next block over there was a dress shop. I stopped and stared, mesmerized by the display in the window. The quality of the work was astounding. I knew for sure it had been magically enhanced, much like I did with my own creations, but I'd never seen anything quite like those dresses before. They were clearly holiday attire, the sort of thing one might wear to a party. I told myself they were intended for New Year's so I didn't get maudlin and walk away.

"Bet I could make one like that. Better, even." I smirked at my translucent reflection in the glass, imagining myself wearing the shimmering copper garment on display. "And I'll make it for a different holiday, one I actually like."

"I bet you can't."

The sudden voice made me spin on my heel. Salem after dark—dangerous, remember? But it was only a guy I'd met before. Someone Aliyah knew. A townie, changeling if I remembered correctly. He was my age, attending Gallows Hill instead of Hawthorn because he wasn't a magus.

We stood gazing at each other. I remembered his face but not his name yet. His eyes were wider than I'd ever seen them, partly obscured by the ruddy hair hanging over his brow. Dude needed a haircut. His clothes were worn, too. Not shabby; I could tell they'd had quality once. They must be for working in at something distractingly physical.

I realized he was startled and probably recognized me, maybe in the same boat trying to remember my name. And just like that, his glamour slipped, and I recalled it. He had the pointy ears and dusky skin of a Goblin, and he was part of a big family here, the Ambersmiths.

"Azrael?" I got ready to ask him loads of questions, which was my default. That way I didn't have to talk about myself or my misery, which was present in abundance that evening.

"In the flesh. Mostly." He held up a bandaged hand.

"What happened?" I blinked. "You didn't cut anything off, did you?"

"Almost. I'm just nearly Fingerless Az." He chuckled. "I got into a fight with a pair of pinking shears in the shop. Not that one, though." He jerked his chin at the window I'd been looking at.

"You know what pinking shears are?" I smiled. Nobody at Hawthorn had the same passion for crafting that I did.

"Yep." He smiled back, revealing front teeth that reminded me of Lune's. The tension in my shoulders faded.

"How?"

"I'm making the rounds as an apprentice to my various family members. It's totally an Ambersmith tradition. Also, I'm pretty sure Aunt Marjorie is going to tell me to look elsewhere when our agreement ends."

"What does she do?" There I went with the questions again.

"Marjorie does home decor. Curtains, tapestries, lampshades—you get the picture."

"Have you worked here yet?" I jerked my thumb at the shop behind me.

"No, not yet." He shook his head. "But it's on the docket for the summer. That's when they make most of this stuff, you know."

"Yeah, I know." I nodded. "The fashion industry has to work two seasons ahead in order to get everything done in time."

"You know an awful lot about that. Are you a dressmaker back in Canada?"

"You remembered." I wiped that smile right off my face because this dude was dangerous with a capital D. I was cautious around people who paid too much attention. Distraction was my jam. "But no, not professionally. I just made stuff for my cousins and me."

"Would you like to see the workshop in there?"

I stopped, staring at Azreal Ambersmith. He'd offered me the equivalent of a day trip to Eden without even realizing it, but I couldn't take him up on it, because then I'd owe him. Don't get it into your head that I assumed he'd want some weird sexual favor either. What he'd expect was conversation, sincerity, and details I wasn't ready to be honest about outside a therapist's office at this point.

"That would rock, but I kinda have to go back to school now."

"Okay, some other time, then." He met my gaze, which I admit, must have been pretty intense just then. Dylan, who favored distraction almost as much as I did, would have looked away, but somehow, this townie didn't.

His eyes were clear and untroubled despite sustaining an injury that could have lost him an appendage—and facing down a magus bold enough to be out alone after dark. Changelings our age weren't much different from humans, besides the glamour. This was a guy who knew the risk and somehow didn't fear it. I was speechless over this. Nearly breathless, too.

Because I didn't want to go back to campus.

"Oh, yeah, another time." I started walking because I had no other choice.

"I'll walk with you. It's dangerous to go alone."

He had no idea that the opposite was also true. That the heart sustains the cruelest wounds, and it was just as dangerous going together.

Especially on Christmas Eve

CHAPTER SIX
ALIYAH

I woke up in January on Sunday morning before the first day of my second semester at Hawthorn Academy. When I packed, I included outfits for social engagements. We'd have another one this semester, though Parents' Night wasn't a thing in the springtime.

Since I was on the Bishop's Row team, I also had a uniform, which was shipped to my house the week of Hanukkah. I took it out of the drawer and ran my fingers over the shiny purple fabric. It had my last name in white on the back, plus my number, fifteen. I laid it flat on the bed and stood staring at it, still awed about making the team. Ember peered down from her perch on the headboard.

"Peep." She opened and closed her mouth a few times, a new gesture for her. Usually, it meant she was curious about an object. I'm pretty sure she'd picked that up from Gale.

"Go on ahead and check it out, girl." I figured the worst she could do was chew on it a little. There was plenty of time to throw it in the wash if that happened.

I folded up the white shorts and purple knee-high socks that went with the top, stowing them in the larger suitcase. I didn't bring the mint green dress this time, and the plum was still at school, hanging in the closet on Grace's side of the room.

Speaking of my roommate, I'd managed to make it into the school to visit her during the break, bringing along a gift for Winter Solstice, which was what she celebrated. Grace was doing okay, although she was sick of hanging around with Nurse Smith, who she called "that Nosy Parker." But her eyes had been brighter, her smile easier, and her shoulders more relaxed. Grace thanked me for the gift—a matching set of throw and neck pillows, and cozy socks. She also had Lee and Dylan for company most of the time, which they split between the gym and the library.

Dylan worked over the break, of course. Mostly in the kitchens, although the Ashfords had him bring Gale to help them with cleaning the library for a few days. I didn't see him or Grace until New Year's Eve when I met them at the Witch's Brew. We made caffeinated toasts to the secular turn of the year, during which I prayed silently for Grace to have a smoother time this semester.

Lee came by our house a number of times, mostly with Izzy. Apparently, they'd spent some time together on their own, according to Cadence, although they had an extremely platonic vibe going on. The mermaid had her own things to do, though, and didn't talk about them. Maybe over the summer, she'd let us all in on what had been happening at Gallows Hill. I'd have asked Brianna, but she got stuck working doubles at Walgreens all the way through break. Retail at that time of year is intense. Azreal was in the same boat with his cart and the Ambersmith's storefronts.

I wasn't entirely sure where Hal went while school was out. He wasn't on campus much, though. Lee tried to find out but had little success. His father was around, popping by while I visited in the lounge. It was a relief that he'd stuck around, making his presence known to my friends and the kids in other years who'd stayed for the break. The headmaster had a benevolent presence, even if he came across as mildly intimidating. We'd all much rather have seen Hal, of course, but every time we asked where he was, Headmaster Hawkins answered vaguely.

I wondered if he'd gone to see his mother. Most custodial arrangements allowed for visitation on holidays, and it made sense for a kid who hadn't been feeling well to want his mother. All the same, each of us worried about him in our own way during his absence.

My mind moved its focus back to the present, where I tried to decide between three dresses for the two semiformal events at school this semester. As I stood there waffling between a turquoise maxi dress, a black and orange floral A-line, and a yellow Empire waist with a hi-low hem, there was a knock at the door.

"Noah, go away." He hadn't bothered with me much over the break, but he freaked out about clothes any time we went someplace.

"I'm not Noah."

"Mom. Come in."

She stepped inside and closed the door behind her. I turned to see that she held a garment bag, one with no small amount of dust on it. It must've come from the utility closet in the basement because there was no way anything in her closet would get into that state.

"I thought I'd come in while you were packing and show this to you. See if maybe you'd like to bring it."

I shrugged. "I can't decide, so yeah, why not? I'll have a look."

Mom hung the garment bag on a hook by my desk. It was over the trashcan, which was good because when she opened the bag, dust fell off it. Mostly in the trash, thank goodness. I stopped worrying about any of that moments later when she unveiled the item inside.

"Wow." I gasped. "Where did you get that?"

"Actually, from Bubbe." She removed the dress from the hanger inside the bag, carefully easing the bottom of it out to avoid getting dust on it.

She held the garment up to the light, and I saw why she'd brought it up here. I stood with my mouth wide open in awe and wonder. It was almost impossible to imagine a time when my grandmother would've worn a dress like this.

"It's gorgeous."

That was an understatement. The pale-pink satin fabric on the bodice was embroidered with golden thread and accented with amber beads. The bottom of the dress must've been dipped in red dye and allowed to hang, giving the fabric an ombre effect. The deep red faded to rust, then russet and salmon as it moved up the skirt. A wide metallic copper ribbon graced the waist. The entire thing reminded me of a sunrise, all the rosy colors of dawn.

"Do you want to bring it to school?"

"I'm not sure." I was instantly worried about how things tended to go sideways for me at school but didn't feel like discussing it now. "I mean, should I even wear something like this? It's too nice. Does Headmaster Hawkins really intend for us to get this dressed up?"

"Do you know your grandmother wore it in her first year there?" Mom grinned. "And she lent it to me."

"No. I wouldn't have imagined." Her statement was nearly impossible to fathom. "How did that happen?"

"It's a long story." She sighed, but in a good way, like she reminisced about something good. "Suffice it to say, your father wasn't going to wear it, and Bubbe doesn't like waste."

"That makes sense."

I thought about how my grandmother treated the friends I brought home, always welcoming them. Even sticking up for Logan in a big way. Considering that, it wasn't so hard to imagine, although I had no idea what things were like for my mother back then. Were the Hopewells like the Pierces, or more like the Fairbanks?

I had a closer look at the dress, noting that there was a tag sewn into the back by hand. It was yellowed with age but easy to read since the lettering was embroidered in the same thread as the designs on the dress. "Ambersmith Fashions?"

"Yes. Michael's grandmother was a dressmaker, and she made this specifically for Bubbe."

"Wow. It must've cost a fortune." I shook my head. Maybe I shouldn't bring it after all.

"Not really. Back in those days, the extrahuman community was extremely tightly knit. They did an awful lot of barter, and your great-grandfather took excellent care of all the Ambersmiths' familiars. All it cost was kindness."

"Do you think it will fit?" I wanted nothing more than to wear this dress and come walking down the stairs at school, maybe even dance in it awkwardly with my friends. But it seemed too good to be true.

"Why not try it on and find out?"

My mother's smile reminded me of all the times she'd helped me with my homework in elementary school, like she knew something I didn't. This dress had been made by extrahumans for extrahumans. For all I knew, it was downright magical, aside from its appearance.

I nodded. Mom turned her back, giving me privacy as I changed into the dress. When I slid the sleeves up my arms, at first I thought they'd be too big, but once I reached behind me to pull the zipper up, I realized that wasn't the case.

This garment fit like it had been made for me. I'd never worn anything quite like it, something that felt so precisely tailored to my particular shape. My eyes stung slightly, and my vision misted over. Mom turned around at that moment.

"Aliyah? Are you okay?"

I had the best mom in the world. There I was wearing this work of art, and the first thing she thought about was my feelings. Which weren't the greatest, I guess, at the moment. And because she cared and always had, I could speak freely about them.

"Maybe not. I mean, I love this dress. Who wouldn't? It's the most amazing thing I've ever tried on in my life." I sniffled, trying not to actually cry. "But the fact of the matter is, I don't have a boyfriend. I'd only be going with friends to probably both of the dances this semester, so it seems like a waste."

"Oh, Aliyah." She held out her arms, and a moment later, I was in them. "There's no such thing as 'only' when it comes to true friendship. Platonic love is still love, and it makes more of a difference in life than society gives it credit for."

"Really?" I sniffled again. "Two of my friends are practically engaged to each other already. I don't want to miss out on dating because everyone makes such a big deal about romance."

"It's a big deal at your age because it's new." Mom stroked my hair. "Dressing up is something you can do for yourself at any age. That's the way it was for Bubbe. Back when she was a first year at Hawthorn, she didn't have a boyfriend either, and she wore that dress."

I blinked, surprised. It was practically a legend in our family, how much my grandmother loved her husband, the man she'd cared for unconditionally for so much of her life. It had never occurred to me there was a time in her life before she met him.

But then I stopped and considered this further. Bubbe was independent, strong, and lived her life the way she felt was right. If she'd been that way since she was sixteen, then it made complete and total sense. Hawthorn Academy was a fancy school. Why wouldn't she wear a fancy dress? I can't imagine my grandmother limiting herself over something as incidental as having a date. Maybe I should do the same.

"Do you think you'll bring it, then?"

I couldn't answer my mom. It wasn't that I didn't want to. She deserved an answer because after this winter, I was aware how lucky I was to have a mother like her. But if I started talking, I'd say too much. I might have started wondering out loud what was wrong with me, why I didn't seem able to have romantic feelings about any of the unattached boys.

I might even have said I was jealous of my friends, and I didn't want to say that out loud. It'd be almost as bad as setting the cafeteria on fire, just in an emotional way. And it could get worse than that. My inside voice might even push me farther down the road toward becoming an out-of-control extramagus.

I stood up straight again, easing out of the hug, partly because I needed to see her face in case I did speak my secret aloud by accident. It was also really not fair to take up her whole day with this. She was Noah's mother, too, and what if he had his own problems?

So I nodded. Mom seemed mollified, or maybe she recognized inner turmoil when she saw it and understood. Either way, she asked me to put my regular clothes back on while she got a fresh garment bag.

After changing, I went about the business of packing all the essentials in my suitcase: Regular clothes, some extra pillowcases and sheets, and of course, the contraband communication orb. I wouldn't go back without that, because it had been a lifesaver last semester. Hal's dad had changed an awful lot at Hawthorn Academy already. Maybe I should ask him to reconsider the no-communication policy. I still took pains to hide it in the small suitcase underneath stuff like underwear that no one would look through.

I decided to bring the turquoise maxi dress, along with Bubbe's. It didn't hold a candle aesthetically, of course, but it was comfortable, I liked it, and the color was soothing, like my tankini. I decided to toss that in too because maybe this semester, I'd join Faith in her weekly swims. Increasing my physical activity would only help prepare for the tournament.

Since we were allowed to arrive on campus anytime on Sunday or even early Monday, I didn't rush through my day. I spent some time downstairs in Bubbe's office, playing with the critters who felt up to it. None of them were strays or otherwise unattached, although a few were in for medical care. Over the holidays, some extrahumans boarded their pets and familiars while traveling overseas.

I thanked Bubbe for lending me her dress, and she seemed glad that I had taken her up on the offer. She asked for pictures if I decided to wear it.

Upstairs, I had breakfast and lunch with my parents. Noah was there too but didn't participate in the conversation. Either he was nervous about going back to school or tired. He had been out an awful lot over the break, making me wonder if he'd started seeing a boy in town. It didn't seem like there were many romantic prospects for him at Hawthorn. I think Darren was the only other gay man on campus.

I'd have to remember to ask him how the old dating life was. Maybe my brother even had some advice. Noah knew more about romance than anyone in my year. Then again, he was guilty of attempted matchmaking in the case of Logan and me, so maybe not.

Talking to Cadence might have been a better idea, although her advice on most things was usually just do it. I wasn't talking about sex; I mean like speed-dating. That was just not my style. I felt like I had to know someone before I could decide if I wanted romance. It had been difficult enough going with Logan to Parents' Night because I'd only known him for a month at that point.

My thoughts were cut off when my parents said it was time for us to go. They asked one more time if either of us wanted to stay the extra night and go to school at breakfast time, but my brother and I both said no. So, we all headed out, walking down the snow-lined streets. There wasn't much coating the ground, just enough to be a slippery nuisance for the suitcases.

The cobblestones on Essex Street were even harder to navigate now than in the fall. I was glad we all went this time. Mom and Dad stayed outside.

The lobby was mostly deserted when we arrived. I looked across it at the stairway, knowing I should go up to my room first and drop off my luggage, but I missed my friends. I had seen most of them over break, but it felt like longer.

They weren't in the lounge or the cafeteria, so I figured they must be upstairs. I should have just gone. Noah already had since the stairs were still moving. I got on, stating my floor. Once they stopped, I walked down the hall toward my room, whistling. When I put my hand on the flat space next to the door, the latch clicked. Inside, I heard frantic rustling and low voices. I stepped back from the door and waited before opening it.

I stood in the hall, counting seconds. One Mississippi, two Mississippi, three Mississippi. Once I got to ten, I opened the door and rolled my suitcases ahead of me. Ember swooped in over my head, flying directly to her preferred perch on my footboard.

Dylan and Grace sat on her bed. They were both rigid, perfectly still, barely even breathing—and their cheeks were flushed. I didn't bother looking at their clothes, because I'd heard plenty from out in the hall. Some adjustments must have happened, since my whistling had signaled someone approaching.

"I'm going down to the lounge for coffee. Once I put these suitcases down, anyway." My back was turned as I tried to compose my face. I don't know what I looked like, but if the heat I felt from the neck up was any indication, I didn't want them to see.

Everything swam: light, sound, the cool air around my flushed face. There was a rush too, the kind I got the year I had walking pneumonia and collapsed on the stoop outside my house. It was nearly impossible to swallow past the lump in my throat, so I cleared it instead, trying to breathe. I managed enough respiration to blurt a question.

"Did you guys have dinner yet?"

Talking about food seemed like the safest topic. My stomach felt like someone clenched it in their fists and squeezed, and Ember's silence spoke volumes. Usually she'd peep at Grace and Lune and Gale and Dylan, but mum was the word for my dragonet.

"Um, no." Grace managed an answer. "I'll meet you down there in a few minutes."

"Sure, no problem." But it was. It shouldn't have been.

I called for Ember and waited until she perched on my shoulder before leaving the room. Then I closed the door behind me, letting it latch. I probably wouldn't see either of them in a few minutes. Maybe not even for a few hours. I wasn't sure what I interrupted, but I had the general idea.

It felt totally wrong to want something Grace had, especially when she had no home and family. I had to stop it now, even if it meant distancing myself from Dylan.

You're powerful. You deserve whatever you can take, even from other people.

"Might does not make right," I muttered to the empty hallway. "Sit down, shut up, and let your friends have what little happiness they can get."

Downstairs, I settled down in the lounge with coffee and biscotti. Lee joined me, and his mild yet comforting presence helped me calm down. Eventually, Logan arrived, hurrying out of the hallway with a backpack and rolling suitcase. Doris paced behind him, and it was clear neither of them was in a good mood.

I stood and sprinted to catch up with him, Ember swooping along behind me. He headed straight for the stairs, and I recognized this tunnel vision from Lab. He was hyper-focused on getting himself and his luggage upstairs and out of sight, but after Grace's near-collapse at the end of last semester, I wasn't about to let Logan deal with whatever this was alone.

"Hey, do you want some help with that suitcase?" I didn't want to make this about his mood unless he wanted it to be.

"No, but company's cool." I got on the stairs with him, and we rode up in silence. At the top, he spoke again. "Aliyah it's terrible. Mom and Dad almost turned me around at the airport and put me on a plane back the second they saw Doris. They were horrible every day. They keep saying I broke our family, ruined their plans for our future. Even Elanor acts like she hates me now, and I don't know what to do."

Logan's voice was strained, cracked, under pressure. His eyes were rimmed with red too, in lines so perfect they could have been drawn by a makeup artist. His hands shook so much he ended up grasping the straps on his backpack until his knuckles went white. My friend needed a lifeline.

"Listen, if anything like that happens again, let them turn you around. Call me. I'll tell Bubbe. She said you're always welcome, right?"

"Thank you." His back was toward me, his head down as he opened his door. I already knew Dylan wasn't in the room, so I followed Logan inside.

We spent some time putting his clothes in the dresser and the wardrobe. This wasn't due to any immediate need to unpack, but it gave him some time to realize he wasn't at home. Instead, he was at school, surrounded by friends.

We all were. Now all we needed to do was navigate the rest of the semester without making any more mistakes.

CHAPTER SEVEN

"Mind if I sit here?"

I looked up, blinking at Alex. It was Lab, and usually Hal was my partner. It'd been that way for all of last semester and all of January. But Hal was late. He had been through the entire first week of February.

"Sure, I guess." I wasn't sure why, except I was tired of rushing through all of our experiments. It wasn't like Alex had gone out of his way to hang out with me since last semester. Maybe Faith had been wrong about him liking me, or maybe he'd found somebody else over the break.

Alex set down his bag and started rummaging through it. Bailey took one look at where he sat, then pouted and stomped off to team up for the lesson with Logan.

I doodled in my notebook, letting my mind wander. Hal Hawkins hadn't been well. He had low energy, shortness of breath, his skin was ashy and dull, and he'd barely done any magic except at Gym during drills. Professor Luciano even infused his materials in Lab.

If he were a critter, I'd have brought him to Bubbe right away. Nurse Smith knew what he was doing, but Hal didn't seem to get any better no matter how much time he spent in the infirmary, and that was a considerable amount this semester.

For the last two weeks, he'd brought his to-go bag down to the infirmary instead of the lounge. Faith had joined him every single night, diminishing our group by two. We missed having them around. Of course, the best solution was for all of us to go down there. Don't think we hadn't tried it.

Nurse Smith had turned all of us away, even Lee, who claimed he needed to talk to him about roommate stuff. Only Faith was allowed to remain, something about how school was stressful, and our friend needed his rest. But nobody said why.

The medicine I studied with Bubbe wasn't specifically for extrahumans, but bodies with magic had plenty in common. The rest of us were stressed and weren't stuck in bed for extra hours each day. Hal Hawkins should have been on the mend by then. He shouldn't have been adding trips to the infirmary to the break between class periods.

Unless there was something seriously wrong with him.

One of the drawbacks of being in our group was that we didn't hear much gossip. Sometimes I wished Cadence went here because she'd tell us everything, even stuff we'd want to unhear later. But hadn't I called the guy sitting right next to me Switzerland? He visited just about every circle of friends in this place. Maybe he knew more about this than we did.

"Alex, what you think is up with Hal?"

"What you mean?" He locked eyes with me, which was a little unnerving, maybe because he had a basilisk for a familiar. I had no reason to think he was hostile or otherwise someone to fear.

"He's been sick all semester." I tapped my pen on the paper. "And I'm worried about him because he's my friend."

"Oh." He shook his head. "I don't know for sure. All I've got are rumors, stuff overheard from upperclassmen. Repeating that isn't always the best idea."

"I think I'm smart enough to take gossip with a grain of salt." I wasn't totally honest, but nobody ever solved a mystery by refusing to ask questions.

"Fair enough." Alex glanced at the door, probably to make sure Hal hadn't just walked in. He was pretty sharp when it came to people, apparently. "Last year, Hal collapsed on his campus tour. Before that, everyone thought he was just a regular space magus like his dad, who taught second year here before the old headmaster left. But the third years had a theory about the other side of his family."

"Go on."

"Students here now never met Mrs. Hawkins. Hal's parents got divorced, and she hasn't set foot on this campus since, but Darren told me his sister, who graduated two years ago, heard she was a Dampyr." He shrugged. "I know next to nothing about them, so that's about all I can tell you."

Maybe Alex didn't know much about Dampyr, but I did. They were the offspring of two vampires, and extremely rare. Back before the Reveal and its early days, they'd often get abducted by extrahuman traffickers. From infants to elders, it didn't matter.

They had high value as blood dolls because their entire biology was different from the humans they resembled so closely. Their blood was the most potent nourishment for vamps, so of course, a woman married into such a high-profile family like the Hawkins wouldn't go around advertising her heritage.

She might even have kept her status a secret from her husband, but that had risks. Dampyr genetics were wonky, making it risky for them to have kids with anyone besides another Dampyr. Their offspring were born with magical maladies that had no cure and only experimental treatments.

Since Hal had a mysterious health condition that wasn't getting better, maybe there was some truth to the rumor.

And if it was correct, he might have qualified for experimental treatment in one of the many medical trials down in Boston. None of them were cures, but according to the medical journals in Bubbe's office, they improved quality of life.

Hal might want to try something like that, but he'd need proof he had Dampyr blood.

There was a fairly simple blood testing substance, one also used in extraveterinary medicine for identifying blood-borne illnesses in magical critters. I'd been helping Bubbe with those for the last few years, and she knew how to run the test and read the results. It wouldn't be official coming from her or even Nurse Smith—you needed a medical doctor for that—but with an unofficial test, he'd know where to go from there.

Bubbe had loads of them in her office. If Hal's problem came from his mom's biology, I might be able to help him find out, but I'd need to smuggle a testing kit on campus and also Hal's permission.

Permission? He's sick. Help him out and just do it anyway. You've got the power. Use it.

It felt like my heart stopped. The voice, the one trying to convince me to do the wrong thing, actually made sense. But it couldn't be the right thing, not coming from this part of my brain. Was this how Uncle Richard had felt? Did he have a devil on his shoulder, too?

"Thanks, Alex." I nodded. "I'm not sure it helps. I feel pretty powerless about now." Take that, evil inside voice.

"It'd be pretty easy to check on without anyone knowing." Alex's tone was casual, light, nonchalant.

See? This boy speaks sense. Why not hear him out?

"What do you mean?" I blinked. He had no idea I waged war with a voice in my head, and that he was unintentionally on its side.

If we're only trying to help, are we wrong?

I tried thinking one of Bubbe's sayings at it, about how intention's only ever part of the bigger picture. Fortunately, my inside voice stayed where it belonged.

"My mom's a genealogist." Alex leaned his head on his hand. "Most of her work is trying to get people back with their families. You know, folks who got separated during the messes during the Reveal. The Boston Internment, that kind of thing. All I have to do is ask her to check the Hawkins family. It's all public information, just compiled."

I waited for the evil inside voice to chime in, but it was silent. I should have been glad about that. It'd been a thorn in my side since I started hearing it. But I had trouble getting my brain around the ethics of the whole situation. It might have been a moot point, though.

If Alex's relationship with his family was like any of my other friends', I couldn't imagine her helping, but we could team up to do our own research.

"What research, now?" Alex's mouth wore a faint grin.

"Sorry, rampaging inside voice coming outside once again." I sighed. "Story of my awkward life."

"It's cute." The grin asserted itself. "Let me know if I can help, aside from talking to mom. Hal's a good guy, and I don't like seeing him sick either."

"Thanks."

After that, we spent the next twenty minutes of lab time working on our experiment. It wasn't too bad, just obnoxiously slow. We had to do something called titration. It was supposed to identify how much acid was in the magically infused solution we were preparing for use next week. Only one drip at a time could go into the flask, and it was super tedious.

Hal didn't make it to class until half an hour in. Faith was with him, so they started the experiment together. Professor Luciano went over to help them, setting up the burette and the stopcock in its stand. Because Hal's hands were too shaky to do fine motor tasks, which made me feel like a goose walked over my grave—or maybe his—Faith helped him with everything else, including taking notes.

Even though they were behind on the experiment, they managed to finish right before the bell rang. Alex and I were with them right down to that wire. We went over to help because we finished early. As we went about our business, watching one solution drip into the other, Faith gave me major side-eye.

I could tell she wanted to talk, so I jerked my chin toward the hall, letting her know we could chat out there. But Alex headed me off as she walked through the door. I was stuck between the last bench and the exit, caught by the strangely paralyzing weight of his hand on my shoulder.

"It might be a little early for me to ask this, but I figure there's no time like the present." He took a deep breath. "Do you want to go to the Valentine's dance with me?"

"I kind of plan to just go by myself." I shrugged. Not with the shoulder he touched, though. I wasn't entirely sure how I felt about it. "Didn't consider a date."

Why are you lying? Tell him how you feel.

I shook my head. Alex took this as emphasis of my spoken point because nobody would have suspected I was hearing a voice. At least, not anybody as sane as he seemed to be.

"Sorry. I sort of assumed since you went to the Parents' Night dance with Logan, that you might want company. And you guys are obviously not dating, so I figured maybe you were ready to move on?"

He seemed surprised. My reaction hadn't been what he expected, and probably wasn't normal. I couldn't for the life of me imagine what that normal was, anyway. All I could do was stand there, blinking. He let go of my shoulder, too, and I wasn't sure how to tell him he didn't need to, that I didn't mind.

Don't mind. That's interesting.

For the second time that day, the evil voice had a point. Wasn't it supposed to be earth-shattering? When someone who was interested touched you, I mean? The world was supposed to go away. At least, that was what it looked like on TV, and how Noah had described getting together with Darren. They'd held hands, and he just knew everything. That he was definitely gay, and that his as-yet future boyfriend was a total hottie. But apparently, I was different.

You're perfectly normal for an extramagus. Yours is a high and lonely destiny.

"I don't know," I answered both Alex and the voice in my head. Ember alighted on my shoulder. She didn't take up a protective posture. Instead, it seemed like she sought comfort. Or maybe tried to give me some.

"But then again, you're not obviously dating anyone." Alex cleared his throat. "Oh. Are you like my cousin? He's asexual; doesn't go out with anyone, ever."

"I don't know?" I shrugged. Ember craned her neck out so I could see her face, tilting her head so far to the right it almost turned completely around like an owl's.

"This whole conversation got weird, sorry." Somehow, Alex managed to smile. His teeth were the tiniest bit crooked, the angle of his grin canted to the right. Maybe he was just as confused as me. "But would you go with me anyway? As friends?"

"Peep!" Ember broke the tension as usual, and we both laughed. Actually, all four of us, because his basilisk was basically a magical snake, like Noah's Lotan but venomous. Despite that small difference, I knew a serpent's mood when I saw it, so I knew she also expressed mirth.

"So, yes," I finally managed, staring at the floor. "I'll go with you to the dance."

Look up. You owe him at least that much after all your waffling.

I did, by reflex, and almost looked away on principle. Why did I listen to a feature of my mental landscape that was probably the opposite of healthy? But what was done was done.

"Wow." Alex's new smile was practically effervescent. "I expected a no after all that. Thank you."

A throat cleared nearby.

"Yes, yes. You're clearly comporting yourself in a manner befitting a gentleman for once, Mr. Onassis. And I've never doubted you're a well-mannered lady, Miss Morgenstern." Professor Luciano tapped his foot. "Now that the matter of your impending date is concluded, I'd appreciate you vacating my lab if it's all the same to you. Unless you'd like to help me sweep and mop the floors in here?"

There was nothing quite like an impatient professor to motivate a couple of pokey students.

We headed out into the hall, where Faith didn't bother pulling me aside for a chat. She nodded, though without a smile. I couldn't blame her. Hal was a mess and so was she, so I wasn't surprised to see them heading to the infirmary.

Alex sauntered toward the cafeteria, raising an eyebrow at me, but I was definitely not ready to take dinner in there and anyway, I had something other than food on my mind. I headed back down the hall to order from Penelope and Sandy anyway, because it was routine and familiar.

"Where's the rest of the crowd, Aliyah?" Penelope glanced past me down the hall.

"They had plenty on their minds today." I shook my head. "Would you mind giving me a couple of extra soup and sandwich meals? I want to make sure some of them don't forget to eat."

"But of course."

Once the order was filled, I thanked Penelope. I brought the bags to the infirmary, hoping they'd provide a reasonable excuse for visiting. Nurse Smith agreed to let me in on the condition I only stayed for ten minutes.

"Hey, you guys." I sat in the chair at the foot of Hal's bed because Faith was in the one beside it. It reminded me of the time they came to see me while I was in here with Logan.

"What's up, Aliyah?" Faith held Hal's hand in both of hers.

Oh, he's not well at all. Look at the wall behind Fairbanks.

I blinked because I was already gazing in that general direction. The last thing I wanted was for either of my friends to think I was staring at the circles under Faith's eyes or the drawn and dried-out look of Hal's face, but once again, the voice was right. There was a tube, an opaque one, leading from a bleached pine panel on the wall to Hal's right sleeve. It disappeared under his shirt, likely ending somewhere on his chest.

I took a deep breath before speaking, focusing on the words I wanted to let out instead of questions better left unspoken. All of them were things I could ask Bubbe this weekend.

"I'm just checking to see what's going on." I set the dinner bags on the bedside table, not bothering to roll it over the bed. "You've been sick for so long, Hal. My grandma knows a lot of folks in the medical community. Is there's anything I can do to help? Like maybe see if she can get you a referral?"

"No." Hal shook his head. "After all this, Dad wants to bring me to Boston, see some specialists, but Mom won't sign off on the forms. With the custody arrangement, she gets to decide. She only lets Nurse Smith treat me."

"What?" My hands curled into fists, just about the only thing I could do to contain my magic. I was suddenly furious, almost as much as at Charity the first day of school. Even with the effort, my hands warmed up. I lifted them off my lap.

"Don't go nuclear, Morgenstern." Faith's tone was droll, but her back straightened, and she dropped Hal's hand. I felt the energy in the room change, some coalescing around her. And I understood. She was prepared to protect him, even if it meant putting me in the next bed over.

A romance for the ages. If only it weren't doomed to end in tragedy.

"Half a minute." I closed my eyes and counted to five as I took long slow breaths in and out, partly to shut the voice up, but also so I didn't go full solar. By then, my hands felt normal again. "I'm sorry, but that was a total shock and definitely not a pleasant one. Are you serious? Doesn't your mom know how sick you are?"

"I'm not sure. It's a moot point anyway." He closed his eyes. "Because without her consent, I can't see any doctors."

Bet your soul the mother knows. Doomed, as I said, unless you do what's needed, even without permission.

"What about an extraveterinarian?" Take that, evil voice. "Do you need permission for Nin to see one of those?"

"No." He opened his eyes. "But how's that going to do any good?"

"Because Bubbe has her friends around all the time. Lots of doctors at Salem General, some who do rotations in Boston, have familiars in her care. Sometimes, they leave stuff there, screening tests in case Bubbe notices a critter's magus is also not well. So, if you brought Nin in for a checkup—" I tapped my temple. "Do you get what I'm saying?"

"Ha." Faith smirked. "Clever."

"Yeah, I think Nin should definitely get a checkup." Hal's smile was faint and wan but still there. "I'm sure me being so sick has got her stressed out, and you know how Pharaoh's Rats are. Prone to illness when under too much pressure."

"I absolutely do." I nodded and smiled. "Oh, there's one more thing.

Just to try getting extra information. Alex offered to ask his mom for a family tree analysis. For you, both sides."

"Don't tell me you agreed to go on a date with him in exchange for that kind of favor." Faith snorted. "I know you're not scared of playing with fire, but poison should give anyone pause. Even you, Aliyah."

"No, it's got nothing to do with that," I admitted before the evil inside voice got a word in edgewise.

"I hope he doesn't think so." Hal sighed. "Quid pro quo is no fun."

"I'll remember that." I tried on a grin that didn't quite fit, partly because I couldn't imagine what else Alex Onassis would want from a mixed-up girl like me. "Do you want me to tell him to go ahead?"

"Yeah, why not?" Hal locked gazes with me. "My mom never talks about her family. I figure you of all people understand what that's like."

"Yeah, I do." Now I wanted to help him even more.

What you really want is leverage over the headmaster through his son. That isn't empathy, and you know it.

I was about to protest by telling my friends I loved them, but the knock on the door meant it was time to go. Nurse Smith was a stickler about the ten-minute limit, so I said goodbye and headed back to join the others in the lounge. Alex was there, and I told him to go ahead with the genealogy. Dylan overheard that but said nothing. At the time, I believed he thought it was for me about Uncle Richard.

Later on, my way up the stairs, he caught up with me and turned all my ideas upside-down.

"What are you doing with Alex Onassis?"

"Why is everyone asking me that?" I stepped to the side, trying to get past Dylan, but he didn't play reverse point for nothing.

"He just doesn't seem like your type." He blocked me. "Because you're, well—"

"I'm what?" I planted my feet and put my hands on my hips. This jostled Ember from her power nap on my neck.

"You wear your heart on your sleeve, Aliyah." He stood in the middle of the hall, taking up more space than I'd ever expected he could, like he expanded to fit it somehow. "You care too much. You commit your whole heart in just about everything you do, and I don't want to see you get hurt."

"I don't want to sound like a bitch, but it's none of your business what I do with Alex." My voice lowered because I wished it were his business. But it wasn't, so the only thing I could do was call him out on it.

"Guess what, you don't sound like a saint." Gale reared up on his shoulder, turning his head to blink at me. "I'm just trying to warn you. He's not into commitment. Not even having it around, generally speaking."

"Get specific then." I tossed my head. "If I wanted vague advice, I'd go see Izzy."

"I can't." He pressed his lips together. They're full, so they didn't make a thin line like Noah's do when he got confrontational.

"Why not?" I raised my eyebrow, feeling totally ridiculous. Of course, good-natured, confrontation-avoiding Dylan Khan could only get into a fight with a Hopewell.

"You know, for someone who's trying to save the world all the time, you're oblivious to personal danger." For the first time, I noticed his hands clenched in tight fists, a mirror of my own, like he was holding something in himself back. "Everybody else sees right through him."

"For someone trying to help, you're awfully insulting." My eyes widened, nostrils flaring. "Last time I checked, you were the world's biggest advocate of neutrality. So, if that's all you've got to say about Alex, stop talking." I palmed the panel next to my door, opening it.

"Ask Noah about your new boyfriend sometime."

I walked inside without saying another word, but that last bit Dylan had said made me curious. Not the boyfriend thing since it wasn't true, but dropping my brother's name. I could definitely talk to Noah and ask what he thought of Alex. Maybe Dylan knew a secret that wasn't his to tell, but Noah might not have that sort of restriction.

"Of course, you've got nothing to say now."

My empty room didn't answer, of course. Neither did the evil inside voice—another sign it wanted to corrupt me, not help. Did all extramagi go through this? I'd have to check in the unlikely event there are books in the library on the subject when I got the chance. *If.*

I brought Ember with me to the bathroom, letting her splash around in the baths while I got ready for bed. Over the week, I tried to find time to talk to my brother, but the opportunity didn't present itself before Friday's dance.

CHAPTER EIGHT

On the day of the dance, I was with Grace, carrying our dinner bags upstairs because both of us were sort of nervous. I wasn't sure what had my roommate in such a bundle of nerves because she and Dylan had been a thing for six months now, but there you go. I guess like stage fright, official and formal date anxiety was something that never totally went away.

Just as we stepped off at the top, I saw something waving at us from the bottom of the stairs. No, someone. I stopped and turned around.

It was Faith. She had Kitty with her, and they alternated between looking over their shoulders and up at us. I got the impression Grace and I were a train they wanted to catch.

"Hang on, Grace." My roommate turned and saw what I did. She nodded and leaned against the banister to wait.

They got to the top and trotted past us, tugging at our sleeves before turning the corner. We followed them, and I noticed they also had their dinners. Hurrying down the hall, we headed toward their room. Grace kept going, but I paused.

"How are we going to get ready without our clothes?" Everyone knew what I meant, so I didn't bother elaborating.

"Aliyah, you can't be out here." Faith's whisper was so loud she shouldn't have bothered with it.

"I'll drop my dinner bag and grab our stuff." Grace patted me on the shoulder. "Don't worry, I'll remember the shoes." She glanced at Faith. "Unless you think I can't be out here either."

"No, you'll be okay." Kitty palmed the plate beside her door, and it unlatched. She pulled it open and gestured inside. "Go get it, and when you come back, do this knock."

Kitty demonstrated a series of raps and taps complicated enough to be Morse code. For all I know, it was. I never learned any. My roommate handed me her dinner and I walked inside with Faith, looking over my shoulder at Grace as she went back down the hall.

The lights came up and I blinked. This dorm room was the same shape and size as my own, but all the furniture had been moved around. Grace and I had decided to keep things simple and leave the beds, desks, and such as we'd found them on arrival.

Faith and Kitty totally redecorated. They'd opted to stack their beds to make bunks. This gave them way more room, and one of them had brought in a long rectangular table from somewhere. It'd been set up like a vanity, with one of the standard-issue mirrors propped against the wall lengthwise along its top.

Their desks sat back to back as a unit with one end against the same wall as their beds. The dressers and wardrobes flanked the vanity table. The whole set up left space in the middle for yet another purloined table, this one round. It had four stools around it that looked suspiciously like the ones we used in Lab.

I scratched my head at first, wondering how in the world they'd gotten all the extra stuff up here or managed to move the heavy wardrobes and dressers around. Then I realized it must have been Hal. He was a space magus and could easily have moved all sorts of stuff just by expending a little energy. He'd have had enough at the beginning of the school year, but it must've taken him a few weeks, even back then.

Looks like love put your old pal Hal on his deathbed. Are you sure all this empathy for your friends and family is good for your health?

I stood in the middle of the room, wishing the evil inside voice away. It had been silent since Monday, and I'd hoped it was away on a long vacation. Or maybe a permanent one. But no, it was back—with a major beef against the Hal/Faith ship staying afloat, apparently.

I closed my eyes, imagining myself setting it on fire, but all that came to mind was solar magic. Opening my eyes, I shook it off, and I had that maddeningly catchy Taylor Swift song stuck in my head. Thanks, evil inside voice.

You're welcome.

Sighing, I set the dinner bags on the table. Following Kitty's lead was probably for the best. She clearly used this table for something other than food most of the time, because there were a few notebooks on top of some hardbacks that looked vaguely familiar. I lifted one to check out the covers.

"Truncheons and Flagons?" I smiled. "I used to play this with some of the kids in town a few years ago."

Yes, until Azrael tried telling Izzy he loved her. More of your life ruined by romance.

"Get out of town?" Kitty laughed. "No wait, don't. Faith, why didn't you tell me Aliyah played?"

"I didn't know." Faith's deadpan delivery exploded into sarcasm the moment she dropped me a wink. "You're pretty mysterious, you know."

I blinked because I never would've thought of myself that way. I felt like my life was an open book, and had totally agreed with Dylan when he said I wore my heart on my sleeve. But transparency like that wasn't specific on stuff like hobbies, especially the ones I'd had before coming here.

We heard the series of knocks at the door, and Faith let Grace in. My roommate carried both of our garment bags and our dressier shoes, which she hung on the wardrobe doors and set by the door respectively. She also brought my makeup case, but nothing like that for herself. Grace never seemed to wear or even own any makeup. I didn't think she needed it anyway.

She disagreed, especially after the Parents' Night dance when she saw a photo of herself and declared she looked washed-out, which was why I'd brought the entire eye and lip sampler pack I got on Hanukkah, which included the inevitable shades that didn't remotely go with my complexion. Surely Grace could find something that worked for her in there.

Apparently, she liked Truncheons and Flagons too because she stared at the books like they were unicorns. Which are definitely mythical, by the way. Bubbe's told me millions of times not to bother looking for one.

"With this many erased notes, there's no way you're in the planning stage." Grace snorted. "So I guess you guys have a game running."

"You'd guess right." Kitty giggled. "What do you think we do when you guys are in the lounge half the night?"

"I had no idea it was something this fun." Grace smiled. "But isn't studying important too?"

"Oh, we study, all right." She picked up a stack of homework, moving it from the table to her desk. "Usually in the library right after Lab."

"So, are you full?" Grace set dinner boxes out. "Not like this," she said, patting her stomach. "I mean the game."

"Most of the time." She nodded. "But Eston wants to run a side campaign. He gets bored with just playing, but I don't have fun that way. He might need an extra player or two."

Now I understood their outwardly odd-couple relationship. Kitty looked like she could be on a magazine cover, and Eston's whole vibe was beanpole Mensa member. Most magi wouldn't consider them compatible because she was fire and he was water, opposite elements, but they'd bonded over a mundane hobby, so connecting on a magical level wasn't essential for them.

"If we don't want to be late to the dance, we should start dinner." Faith grabbed some bamboo cutlery from the pile she and Grace had made on the table. Then she pulled out a stool and sat down.

"Right." I sat next to her and ate my own dinner, even though I wasn't very hungry. The last thing I wanted was my stomach growling all night long, although it was a fine line between that and anxiety-induced nausea.

"So, what was the whole thing back in the hallway?" I gestured at the door with my fork. "What did you mean? Why can't I be out there?"

Faith swallowed her last mouthful of coleslaw. "Elanor's looking for you."

"What?" I blinked, almost leaning back. It was a good thing I didn't, considering the stool had no back.

"You heard me." Faith pushed BBQ pulled pork around the box it came in. "And she doesn't look happy." She took a tiny bite. Apparently, she didn't have much of an appetite, either.

"Does anyone know why?" I picked up one triangle of my tuna salad on pumpernickel but just stared at it. Even one of my favorites, prepared especially for me because the main offering had no Kosher hacks, didn't improve my appetite.

"Maybe it's got something to do with the fact that Logan has no date." Kitty shook her head. "He's totally fine with going stag, or at least that was what he said on Monday."

"Well, considering she and Noah practically tried to arrange our marriage on the first day of school, I can understand that." The sense this made alleviated some of my gut agitation, so I took a bite of my sandwich, finally.

"I think you might be assuming wrong." Grace talked around a bite of her pork, which she shoveled onto a roll. She realized her breach of etiquette and swallowed before continuing, "Because Logan does have a date. He's going with Hailey."

"I had no idea." Kitty blinked. "I can't believe I didn't hear about that."

"Everyone makes mistakes." Faith grinned, and I nodded in return. I got with her double meaning. "I'm glad he's going with her instead of Bailey, at any rate. Hailey's all but stopped hanging around with Charity. I'd figure both of them would have come around by now. I mean, my sister's only here for a few more months."

I dropped my sandwich because I was still in the dark. "I still don't know why Elanor's on the warpath, guys. Do you think I should avoid her during the dance too?"

Everybody nodded. Uh-oh.

"I'll try to help." Grace wiped her hands on her napkin. Her sandwich vanished. "I'm not sure what I can do, though."

"The last thing any of us needs to deal with is a bunch of inter-year drama." I stared wistfully down at my sandwich because it'd probably go to waste now. "Why do half the upperclassmen give me grief?"

"I don't know." Kitty sighed. "I guess we'll find out if she ever tells us what her problem is. Maybe you won't have to wait too long, but I hope she decides to tell you calmly and in private."

"Right. Because I definitely don't want cafeteria part two, Bonfire Boogaloo."

Everybody laughed, and it was good because they laughed with me. If I couldn't solve a problem, the least I could do was make the best of it. Laughing helped with that, most times.

We finished our dinner, then made use of some cool beauty products Kitty had stashed in her dresser. Her two moms ran a magicpsychic cosmetic company. She got to test all sorts of new gadgets and stuff before anyone else even heard about them.

She gave each of us breath-freshening tablets to put in our mouths. They cleaned teeth as well as a toothbrush, flossing, and mouthwash, but without effort. We just popped one in our mouths and went about other business for two minutes. After chasing them with water, we were all set on the fresh breath front.

I brought out my makeup sampler, and Kitty clapped her hands as she jumped up and down. This kit was part of her family's collection. Lucky for me since I wouldn't have known how to use some of those applicators. They were very different from the mundane cosmetics I'd always gotten in the drugstore.

Kitty also gave us magical cloths for washing our faces before applying makeup. Once we used them, we tucked them into a special container, which used magic and psychic energy to disinfect and infuse them with new cleansing solution.

"How did they ever come up with this stuff?" Grace smiled. "This is amazing. I've never seen anything like them. It must be awesome for the environment too."

"Both my moms graduated from Ellicot City Magitechnic." Which made sense. It was definitely something to be proud of.

ECM was every bit as prestigious as Hawthorn Academy, just for magipsychic technology instead of familiar studies. Noah had looked at applying there before he bonded with Lotan. It was similar to Providence Paranormal in that it had been founded as an alternative to a mundane school. In ECM's case, Baltimore Polytechnic Institute.

Kitty continued, "One majored in botanical sciences and the other in magipsychic chemistry out at Cal Magitech. They learned way more advanced stuff than we do in Lab here. Anyway, extrahumans have been improving skincare with their powers forever, but after the Reveal, they realized there'd be a market for magic cosmetics anyone could use."

"You mean this doesn't take any energy to run?" I picked up the package we'd put the used cloths into. "It's already charged and everything?"

"They keep working for about six months, but then you can send them back to get recharged. My moms have psychics, magi, and faeries staffing an entire department for this sort of thing since even the most powerful magi can't replenish the glamour or psychic energy in these."

"That's so cool." And it totally was. What an amazing world we lived in.

We sat in front of the makeshift vanity, which was long enough to accommodate all four of us, and got glamorized. It was cool spending time with Kitty. I never would've thought she was this interesting just by looking at her. It made me wonder how many other people I'd misjudged or otherwise made incorrect assumptions about every day. The reverse was also true.

The entrance we made for the Valentine's Day dance was nothing like Parents' Night. For one thing, we weren't on the arms of our dates—just a gaggle of girls, friends heading out for a good time. There were two reasons for this.

Without phones or other means of sending instant messages, there was no way to inform the guys when we'd head down to the lobby. That was simple and general and applied to all four of us. But the other reason was just for Grace and me.

The two of us balked, lagging behind Kitty and Faith because we were both more than a little self-conscious about formal socializing. Even though my dress was a literal work of art, and Grace's hand-made one came close, we were still nervous. That was why we held hands on our way down the stairs.

I couldn't look at the crowd or the lights or even think about meeting up with Alex at that point. I was too busy being amazed by my roommate's handwork. Once again, she'd made something to wear during Creatives. It was practically miraculous and made her look like she belonged on the red carpet.

Grace had chosen two types of fabric, one opaque and the other sheer, and combined them into two layers for her dress. The lower was a rich earth-tone orange. I was no expert on textiles, but whatever fabric it was made from moved with her athletic frame, accentuating her natural lithe strength. But the fabric she'd layered over that took the cake. It was bright as a new penny, mesh and lace with a geometric pattern of zigzag lines. The way the long bars caught the light reminded me of strands of beads.

"Your dress is awesome." I grinned at my roommate.

"Said the pot to the kettle." She dropped me a wink. "You know where mine came from. Where'd you get that?"

"It's a hand-me-down from Bubbe." I chuckled. "Would you believe Azreal Ambersmith's great-grandmother made this?"

"I've seen the shop downtown. Do they still make stuff like that, though?"

"I don't know, but I can ask Az next time I see him. Any particular reason?" I immediately thought of one—that Grace might try seeking an apprenticeship with the Ambersmiths in summer. They'd probably accept her based on the Halloween costume alone.

"Not really, just curious. It's interesting how even though we get Creatives, there's no emphasis on actual teaching when it comes to the process of crafting here at Hawthorn."

"Don't look now," I toned my nervous titter back in hopes it'd become a vague sort of chuckle. "But we're sort of being watched."

And we were. By pretty much everyone. While we were talking, the stairs had stopped, depositing us on the main floor. Faith and Kitty had already stepped away toward Hal and Eston, leaving us in prime viewing location for the rest of the folks waiting around for the dance to start.

The first thing I noticed was Noah's dropped jaw. He stared in what looked like abject horror. Maybe he'd seen this dress before, maybe he hadn't, but either way, he freaked out over me wearing it. He stood next to Darren, holding a cup of punch toward him like a peace offering. He didn't move, only stared, so I considered myself safe from whatever level of wrath he had going for now.

The next thing I saw was Dylan. He stood in front of a chair, thank goodness, because his knees collapsed out from under him as he stared. At Grace, I think. He'd literally been swept off his feet, but that was okay. Once she saw him, she was in motion as sure and swift as any she made on the court.

I didn't know what happened next between the pair because Alex was too smooth for the shenanigans plaguing Dylan. He sauntered toward me, all half-smile and twinkling green eyes. His tie was pink because I'd told him that was the main color of my dress. I noticed that as he gave me a flourishing bow, one that might have flattered a marquis at a faerie court gathering.

Until that moment, I had not quite realized how handsome Alex Onassis was. He wasn't pretty like Logan, whose looks were delicate and chiseled. And he wasn't solid and present like Hal, or even quietly charming like Lee. Alex brought to mind those painted pottery shards from ancient Greece, the ones depicting men at the peak of their athletic prime.

While his skin wasn't bronze like the ancient Greeks', its unblemished paleness reflected light like the moon when at apex. He'd done something with his hair, which was normally dark brown with a natural loose curl. Tonight, he'd used some sort of wax to give it highlights with a silver sheen. And there was one more thing I noticed, just as I took the hand he offered me.

"Is that eyeliner?"

"I wanted to look my best." He kissed my hand. "For you."

There was no response I could think of that didn't feel awkward or sarcastic in a way only my friends would understand, so I said nothing, only nodded and gave him the best smile I could muster. That was hard, because Alex went beyond cleaning up well. He was pretty much gorgeous, and it hit me harder than I would've expected. He seemed so plain on a daily basis that this was a huge surprise.

You might think from the way I described Dylan and Logan, and now Alex, that all the guys at my school are hunky, or at the very least endearingly cute. Sometimes, it's more about the moment than anything aesthetic.

We walked along the sides, avoiding the same thing everybody else did—stepping on the dance floor. I mean, really, who wanted to be the first couple to kick off an evening that was supposed to be all about romance? Who wanted everyone's eyes on them that way, so that the person they were with was indelibly linked to them for the rest of their time at Hawthorne Academy?

Faith and Hal, of course.

I won't get flowery and tell you that they stepped lightly out onto the parquet floor, letting their emotions carry them to all sorts of ballroom dancing heights. That would be a lie. Hal was a wreck, after all, and Faith's concern for him, while touching, was the farthest thing from light.

But together they had courage, and that bond let them tread where no one else dared. At the Parents' Night dance, Hal had led our whole group through the event. Although his presence hadn't diminished, he lacked the energy he'd had at the beginning of the year. But they were true partners, probably destined. I knew that when I saw it because of my parents.

Faith rose to this occasion more so than anyone expected, judging by the faces of the upperclassmen and especially her sister. Faith didn't smile to light up a room or even to shame the devil. Instead, it was gentle, kind, and slow, and I realized she was totally brilliant in more ways than one.

There was no way Hal Hawkins could have hoped to keep up with anyone on the dance floor, not without Faith setting the pace on it before anyone else could. Again, like on Parents' Night, this was a waltz, measured steps in a particular and recognizable pattern. It should have worn Hal out, but somehow Faith worked pauses for him where she flourished into the three-quarter time. That put the focus on her so he had space to breathe.

It was heartrendingly touching. My mind kept going back to that tube in the infirmary, the one sticking out of the wall. I didn't know what that tube was, but I knew what was on the other side of it.

The Under. The unending source of magic that we each had access to, depending on our body's ability to absorb it through the barrier between worlds. While an extramagus like me could access more than my fair share, Hal had the opposite problem. His illness must limit his magic.

Clever girl. He's dying, you know.

I almost did something supremely stupid and shouted at the voice to shut up and go away forever, but in the space between the breath I took and the sound I'd have made, Alex spoke.

"Shall we?"

"Yes." The word came out louder and more strident than it might have at a different point in time, but that couldn't be helped. At the very least, Alex knew I was ready to dance. He had no idea about my reasoning, that I needed distraction from a voice in my head. That I couldn't face the likelihood that my friend was dying.

That was how I ended up as part of the second couple on the dance floor at a Hawthorne Academy function. The dress caught everyone's attention, and there I was, the girl who'd always said she couldn't dance.

CHAPTER NINE

This time, the song was *Blackout* by Muse.

It wasn't as easy, managing to waltz. Logan had been good at leading because the Pierces had insisted he learn every dance known to man. He did that with Hailey, who seemed to be enjoying herself. Dylan just goofed his way through it, with Grace playing along. Alex Onassis was neither of those things, not a reluctant performance artist or a class clown. He was a showman.

My date wasn't concerned with taking precise, measured steps or teaching me to waltz properly. What Alex wanted was to show me off, or maybe the dress, or both. Instead of sticking to one corner or even one side, he paraded me around the dance floor like he needed us to be seen from all angles.

I felt like he was on a date with the dress, not me. Anyone could have worn that garment and looked amazing, twirled around in his arms. He was handsome and impeccably well-mannered, but I barely knew Alex and wouldn't know if I had feelings for him until much later. Being considered an ornament didn't bother me. I was okay with that. But also, wrong.

"Everyone's staring in a good way," he murmured.

"No, they're not."

"If that's what you need to tell yourself. But you look stunning, so I'm not surprised."

"It's the dress."

"Do you have any idea who you look like?"

"Do I want to know?" I shrugged one shoulder. "That sort of stuff isn't a big deal to me. This dress was my grandmother's."

"It really isn't the dress, though." He leaned closer, enough so I felt his breath in my ear. "You look like the Sidhe queen."

"No, sir." He was so close I didn't dare shake my head for fear of bumping his with mine. "You can't mean that. Besides, if a changeling ever heard you—"

"Well, you could be related to her." He twirled me, putting some distance between our faces for a moment. "Are you sure you haven't got any Sidhe blood?"

"You know I do." I sighed. "My uncle's a Hopewell, remember?" I refused to refer to my mother as one, but I didn't say that aloud.

"Yes, that's right. I'd forgotten."

No, he hasn't, and you know it. He appreciates these things about you, the ones others would shame you for. Unlike that fool you secretly pine for. And it's something you ought to take pride in.

I continued moving, dancing along and trying not to pay any heed to the evil inside voice. It was awfully flattering all of a sudden, which wasn't typical. I didn't like it.

"Would you like to rest, then? Have some punch, perhaps?"

"No. Just something in my shoe." The quick save wasn't genuine, but at least it was realistic. Thank goodness, because I wasn't sure I could handle all the comparisons in my brain right now.

In case you weren't current with the news, my uncle Richard wasn't just in jail for attacking students at Providence Paranormal College. He was also on trial for crimes against extrahumanity, including a coup in which he'd tried to murder both faerie monarchs. Alex telling me I resembled said royalty right now was more than a little unnerving.

"Are you sure it's a shoe and not that every song is a waltz?" He chuckled, raising an eyebrow. He almost looked like one of the pointy-eared aliens from that series on TV. You know the one.

"Maybe." I managed a smile. If only the evil inside voice would shut up and let me have anything to myself. I didn't want to feel like this. "I'm pretty sure they played most of the same songs on Parents' Night."

"Yeah, but at least it's not *Hide Your Love Away* by the Beatles again." He shook his head. "Yet. The upperclassman say that gets played at every dance in this place."

"Isn't that a little inappropriate for a Valentine's Day dance?"

"Yes and no." His eyes were half-lidded, an expression I'd come to recognize as noncommittal from him. "Perspective rules all."

"Hey, I've got an idea." His comment about perspective helped me realize there was a nearly universal one, and I knew just the song to express it. "Does the DJ take requests?"

"Yes, but only waltzes. That's all they do here."

I shook my head as I led Alex off the dance floor. It felt strange, taking the initiative and changing something even if it was only a school dance playlist, but it was good to actually have an opinion and be proactive with it for once.

Nobody else was over by the DJ's table. I felt downright rebellious.

"I'm guessing most of the students here don't bother with this sort of thing."

"Does that matter to you?" His half-grin lit his whole face somehow.

"No, not at all. In fact, I kind of like this." I smiled.

"It looks good on you. Almost as good as when you get competitive on the court."

I didn't know what to say to that, so I turned away. My face heated up. Alex was mostly a mystery to me, but the one defining feature of our interactions was flattery. Big time. I was out of my depth and wondering whether he knew that.

"Aliyah Morgenstern, what a surprise."

"Zeke?" I blinked. The last person I'd expected to see manning the DJ booth was a vampire CNA straight out of the infirmary.

"The very same." He gave me a half-bow, which was weird coming from a guy wearing scrubs. "How may I help you?"

"If it's not too much bother, I'd like to request a song. I've heard that's not the way things are done here, but there's something I'd like to try dancing to."

"It's been decades since anyone's made a request, but it's not unheard of." Zeke nodded. "However, there's a rule here we both must follow regarding the music."

"Let me guess: I have to select something in three-quarter time."

"Correct." He nodded. "Although six-eight is also acceptable."

"Could you please play *Somebody to Love* by Queen, then?" I wanted to hear this so badly I clasped my hands in front of my chest.

"But of course." He put on a glove to tap the screen in front of him. Vampire fingers didn't register on touch screens, and apparently, his rig was digital. "I'll need to set it up, so you'll hear it two songs after this one that's currently playing."

"Thank you so much."

"You're quite welcome." He gave us the sort of wave most often seen on parade floats. "Have a lovely evening."

I turned, heading toward the punch bowl. First, I glanced around, making sure Charity Fairbanks wasn't watching. The last thing I wanted was for her to try to get revenge for the stunt Hal had pulled on Parents' Night. But she was nowhere to be seen.

"Let me get that for you. You've got to fix your shoe. Right?"

"Oh, yeah." I'd almost forgotten about the quick save. Of course, it came back to haunt me since Alex paid more attention to things than he appeared to. I took a seat nearby, turn my back, and took my shoe off. I went through the motions of pretending to knock something out of it.

You wouldn't have had to lie if your uncle had pulled his gambit off. That pathetic Fairbanks girl wouldn't dare look at you sideways. You'd be related to royalty for real.

I slipped my shoe back on and stomped it on the floor a couple of times, not because it didn't fit. It was pure defiance of the evil inside voice since I couldn't just come out and say what I was thinking where people could hear. I didn't care one bit about what it said anyway, except the part about lying. Did the voice come from all the deceit I'd practiced? I leaned back in the chair, trying to recall the first time I'd heard it, but came up with nothing.

I didn't like lying, but unfortunately, it had become part and parcel of my social landscape here at Hawthorn Academy. And at home. No one in my family had any idea I was an extramagus. How did I go from being a girl who loved the truth to somebody living a lie?

"Here's your punch." Alex sat beside me, handing over a cup. "Drink up before your song comes on."

"Thanks." I leaned back in the chair and took a sip.

The beverage wasn't what I expected. It was tangier than any other juice I'd had before, but maybe that was just the punch flavor at Hawthorn. I wouldn't know from experience since I'd left the welcome ceremony early, and the punch had ended up on Charity's head at Parents' Night.

Go on and laugh. I know you want to.

I listened to the music instead of the voice. Alex had a point. We had maybe half a song left before my request played. I didn't hold my nose, but it was a near thing. I needed to chug this punch or risk missing my dance. I held the cup to my lips and tilted, guzzling it down.

"Whoa, go easy there." Alex glanced at something behind me. His eyes were little wider than usual.

"Too late." I shrugged and handed him the empty cup.

"Okay." He'd gotten stiff and awkward all of a sudden, something I never expected to see on him.

Even on a regular day, Alex was the opposite of a stuffed shirt. He had a rolling gait and a near-constant ease of existence about him in class and at Gym. Practically low-strung. So, I couldn't help but wonder what was going on with him.

Something moved out of the corner my eyes. I turned my head to see Elanor and Noah standing in the doorway from the hall that led to the bathrooms. She held him by the arm as he struggled to pull away. I hoped they weren't fighting since she was his best friend, and he'd been extra moody this semester. He needed her. Finally, she shook her head, speaking words that calmed him somehow.

When Alex returned from disposing of the cups, he immediately took my hand, leading me to the dance floor again. This time he went the long way around, putting distance between Noah and Elanor and us like he was trying to avoid them.

I was about to open my mouth, ask him what was up. He still looked awfully stiff. My vague and frustrating argument with Dylan sprang back to my mind, and I realized the other person who could answer questions about Noah's and Elanor's beef with Alex was the boy himself. But it was too late. I heard the clink of a piano as the song began.

We stepped onto the parquet along with several other couples and even some folks by themselves or in larger groups. Apparently, I had made a popular choice, or maybe it was just that the song felt more upbeat than the others Zeke had played this evening.

As we danced, the floor got more crowded. It seemed like everyone, even the faculty, joined in. I spotted Professor DeBeer dancing with Coach Chen—not a pair I'd have predicted, but it looked like they had fun. Even Professor Luciano was out there with us, doing something that reminded me for all the world of videos Noah had showed me on the internet of a now-shuttered Goth club down in Boston.

By the time the bridge played, the part where the incomparable Freddie Mercury sang about how he was going crazy, I felt practically weightless. If it weren't for all the other people on the dance floor, I'd have felt like I was flying. Ember soared overhead, swooping and dipping in the air along with the music, which enhanced that sense. It was dizzying, almost maddening.

Perhaps you are, in fact, mad. Already. That would be a record, even for an extramagus.

"No." Oops.

"What?" Alex blinked, but his feet didn't miss a step.

"Nothing." All of a sudden, I wanted to get away from him. In my mind's eye, I pushed him away to run off the dance floor and up the stairs toward the sanctuary of my room, but I couldn't. There were too many people there. Familiars, too.

"You can tell me." He spun us, letting centrifugal force pull us closer together.

"I can't." The entire situation, this proximity of our bodies, was untenable.

At least that's true. But you ought to tell him. He might even like it.

"Stop! Stop already. I can't take this anymore!"

I didn't scream, but it was certainly loud to Alex, whose ear was next to my cheek. At that point, I didn't think things could get any worse. Glancing up, I saw Dylan staring at me. Grace, too. And Logan looked away from Hailey, furrowing his brow at me. So, I wasn't exactly quiet either.

Oh, dear, it looks as though I've gone and made a mess. Or rather, you have.

I looked down, expecting to see the floor on fire or something extremely horrific like that. It wasn't quite so bad but still qualified as terrible because my hands glowed. With solar energy.

Not noticeably yet, partly because of the strobing lights but also Alex swinging me out with both of my hands in his. It was about to get worse fast, and if I didn't get out of there soon, the entire school would know my secret.

"Hold on, Aliyah. You can snap out of this. Come on." He gripped my hands, and I felt energy between us. Not just my solar magic but his poison.

I wasn't sure what he expected to accomplish. Solar and poison weren't opposites but not reactive either. So, mingling his energy with mine didn't seem like it'd do much good, but I was wrong.

I felt lightheaded all of a sudden; my feet got stumbly and my breath shallow. I found myself leaning on Alex instead of dancing with him, like the song was a power ballad instead of pleading gospel. I still wanted out of there. I'd have run, but it was all I could do to keep my balance.

I had less control, less agency, here with Alex. I was worse than vulnerable, and even though I'd seen it in movies, it just felt wrong. He diminished me somehow.

The glow started fading from my hands, but the heat remained. Now I wouldn't reveal my secret as an extramagus, but I did have to worry about setting the dance floor on fire. The poison had gone beyond sapping me of strength to conjure solar. It had lost me control of my fire.

"Sorry." Alex's jaw dropped. I'd never seen him this emotional before. "I overdid it."

"It's not your fault. I am what I am." I whimpered, ashamed of the new disaster. "Can't I go a semester without setting stuff on fire?"

"At least you didn't let the sunshine in."

I couldn't move my head without feeling dizzier, so I rolled my eyes to look up at him.

"I figured it out." He gazed down into my eyes. "I think you're incredible."

"You won't feel incredible when you catch fire. I should go." I tried to walk away, but I stumbled.

"Don't." He caught me. He hadn't looked away from my eyes the entire time.

"Why not?" I'd almost have preferred falling on my face at that point. At least I'd have made the effort to leave.

"I can fix this, but it's gonna cost you."

"Anything." All I could think about were my friends and classmates who would get hurt if I couldn't hold back my fire.

"Okay, then." Alex Onassis tipped my chin up, then bent over me, placing his lips on mine.

It was my first kiss, which was disappointing. Like I said, I'd only been interested in one guy so far, and it was not Alex.

As far as kisses went it was fairly tame, at least compared to what I saw on TV and Noah's descriptions. The main purpose in those instances was getting romantic, after all.

What Alex did was all about banishing his element. I suppose I had that going for me, at least. I can honestly say my first kiss was truly magical, even if not in a fairytale way.

Some of the fog in my mind and weakness in my limbs eased. Not all of it, but enough of my faculties returned that I could hold back the fire on my own. But that wasn't the best way to explain it.

Firsts are important because they shake you out of complacency and make you question the way things are. When the shield of the way things have always been slips, you see truth. Because that kiss wasn't romantic, its effect was entirely unexpected.

It gave me a major epiphany about my whole magical situation.

Every time something was unjust or someone got hurt, my fire turned up to eleven. In the cafeteria, I couldn't abide Charity abusing Faith and bullying Noah.

Every time I tried to hide myself, I let the sunshine in. That night on the stairs between Bubbe's office and home, I'd had to conceal that obnoxiously persistent solar magic from my whole family.

Which is exactly why you ought to realize your entire situation is untenable.

"I'm a ticking time bomb."

"You just need an outlet." He patted my back. "Some way to use what you're hiding, where only the people who know can see. Otherwise, it'll only get harder."

"How could you possibly know anything about this?"

"I'm not like you, but my cousin is."

"Oh." I sighed, shaking my head. "All the same, I think it's probably for the best if I leave this dance early."

"Would you like some company?"

"I don't think so. I'm sorry."

"I'm not."

Alex escorted me to the stairs, then waved as I ascended. While nowhere near as triumphant as my exit from Parents' Night with the rest of my friends, at least this social outing wasn't a total failure. I'd managed to escape with everybody unscathed. Well, almost everybody. Because the last thing I saw as I stepped off the top of the moving staircase was Noah shaking his finger angrily at Alex. I couldn't imagine why, but I was exhausted and not going back down there.

It was time for a bath and sleep. The last thing I wanted to do in a state like that was to forget self-care. When you're an extramagus, the worst-case scenario is usually total disaster.

CHAPTER TEN

Alex was right; I needed to use my solar magic to understand it better, so I practiced in small ways, starting the day after the dance. After that, I could contain it a little more reliably. I still ran the risk of accidentally using it at the wrong time, but it was a more conscious kind of mistake, like grabbing grapefruit juice when you wanted orange.

How did I practice something this secret?

I'd taken to turning the lights on and off with my solar magic in the privacy of my own room. I had done it in the bathroom once before too, but Kitty walked in shortly after. That was the end of that.

So far, I hadn't busted out with it in Lab or anything, and as long as I ran laps before all of our Bishop's Row practices, I didn't seem to have a problem in Gym or practice. All the same, it was on my mind all day, every day.

Mundane teenagers worried about acne, bad hair days, and not knowing any of the answers to what's on a pop quiz. I got all that and more, and to top it off, Noah was breathing down my neck. Apparently, he had a problem with Alex and me.

I ended up sort of going out with Alex Onassis. By default, maybe. At the beginning of the year, I couldn't even have told you his last name, and here I was, engaging in an understated sort of couplehood with the last person I expected. Mostly it was no big deal. We walked together in the halls, sat together at lunch. While he didn't have dinner in the lounge with us because of Kitty's Truncheons and Flagons campaign, he visited our booth at the end of breakfast.

We'd held hands maybe twice since the dance, briefly and awkwardly. And we hadn't kissed since then either, which was a relief for me. Kissing was scary, which meant I wasn't ready for more. If that bothered Alex, he didn't show it. The whole thing felt like still needing training wheels on a bike.

Maybe I was being too harsh about it. My parents were my relationship benchmark, and they had serious big love energy. The same was true for Faith and Hal. It'd be unfair to expect something that epic for myself because clearly nobody else had anything like that going on. Not even Grace and Dylan.

Those two spent a good amount of time together, but their familiars practically ignored each other, which hinted at some sort of tension. And I hadn't seen them show any affection since the night I'd walked in on whatever it was they were doing after winter break. They seemed more connected on the Bishop's Row court than at any other time, but that made sense since they shared athleticism.

Their new vibe reminded me of how I was with Logan, which was to say, they partnered in Lab, laughed together over Professor Luciano's far-fetched mnemonic study suggestions, and clowned around. Dylan seemed comfortable with it. Grace didn't. She blasted him with longing stares almost every time his back was turned.

I wanted to talk to my roommate and ask if she was okay. Every time I did, she avoided the subject of Dylan altogether. If I mentioned his name, she made sure the rest of our conversation was all about the tournament, or a quiz, or something cute that Lune did. It wasn't healthy for her to be silent about what bothered her, so I confronted her in the café one Saturday morning.

"Look, Grace. I wanted to sit down and touch base." I reached across the table and grabbed her hand. "You're my friend, and I care. How are you doing?"

"Oh." She blinked, her hand tensing under mine. I couldn't imagine why. "No, I'm hanging in there. I've been talking to the headmaster. He's a licensed counselor."

"Okay." I nodded, my exhale heavier than usual but not enough to qualify as a sigh. I'd gotten sickeningly good at hiding things. "That's good, then. Do you need anything?"

"Well, spring break is coming up in a week." Grace stared at the table. "And I'm not going to my aunt's."

Sometimes, the people who needed help most couldn't take that extra step and ask for it, so I offered.

"Do you want to hang around with me in town? I can ask my mom if you can stay over for some of the break. And Passover is next week. Do you want to come to Seder? There's a full dinner but served with only matzo, no bread. It's traditional but fun."

"That'd be awesome, Aliyah. Thank you."

She asked about the holiday, and I explained that Passover was about remembering times of oppression and celebrating liberation from them. She asked if there was anything she could bring and I gave her the standard answer: an item that symbolized liberation for her. Our conversation continued on, mostly about class.

Once again, she avoided the subject of Dylan, who I happen to know was also staying for break. He'd mentioned it before. He'd also told me that over winter break, he and Grace had spent most of their time on campus together. Grace apparently wanted to avoid him this time.

Maybe it was just being shut up here in the school. The spring weather was much nicer than the frigid temperatures we had at the end of December and beginning of January, and there was more going on in town to boot.

I guess the whole confrontation/intervention thing was going around like the plague because that same afternoon, Noah knocked on my door. I let him in even though it was an enormous surprise for him approach me in the middle of a weekend day. Either Charity was in New York, or he didn't care what she thought anymore. I hoped it was the latter.

No such luck.

"You have to stop seeing Alex." Noah crossed his arms, leaning against the door he'd just closed behind him.

"You don't tell me what to do." I snorted. "You've barely spoken to me all year at school over practically nothing, and now you're trying to dictate my dating life?"

"You don't understand, Aliyah." He closed his eyes.

"Then explain it to me because you coming in here and saying something like that is super rude." And it was, even if I was mostly indifferent about my so-called boyfriend anyway.

"He's poison." Noah opened his eyes but stared at the floor. Lotan slithered out of his collar and rubbed cheeks with him, a sign his familiar knew there was something wrong.

"Tell me something I don't know. Duh, poison magus. That fact's right there in front of me in Lab every day. And in Gym, to boot. You know we're on the team together, right?"

"That's not what I'm talking about." My brother's voice sounded like it came from the bottom of a well. "I'm trying to tell you he's no good."

"You said the same thing about me at the beginning of the semester, and I'm your sister." Ember got between Noah and me, perching on my desk and thrusting her neck out.

"I'm sorry." Noah opened his eyes, and I saw the tears in them. "I thought you'd want all the same things I did out of school. I didn't realize you'd always be different from the crowd I hang around with now, and I let myself think that was more important than you. But nothing is. You're my little sister, and all our lives, I promised to take care of you. I seriously dropped the ball, and it was the biggest mistake I've ever made in my life. Well, almost."

"What you mean by 'almost?'" I froze. "What could be worse? You're not a bad person, so there's no way you could have done something so terrible you're this afraid to talk about it."

He'd been hiding something enormous. I couldn't assume it was the same as mine, though. As much as I'd love to not be alone with my secret, he wouldn't be going on about who I dated if the problem he'd hinted at was being an extramagus.

"It'd be worse if I let you keep dating Alex after what he's done." He took a deep breath and closed his eyes again, as though he couldn't bear to see my face when he told me the truth. "Aliyah, he—"

The door hit him in the back, and he stumbled forward into the room. Noah righted himself, but the moment was lost. There was no way he could finish the sentence now, not with who'd just walked into my room.

Grace wore gym clothes. She had a chest of ankyr and cestus under one arm and wasn't alone. Dylan, Alex, Lee, and Faith all followed her in. My roommate chattered away, totally oblivious to anything besides what she was focused on, Bishop's Row.

"The gym's clear, so I talked to Coach, and she says we can use it. Lee and Faith need more practice in case Coach Pickman takes them off the bench and they're not getting it during the week. So, I figured, since you were just studying up here anyway, we could— Oh."

She saw Noah. Well, she noticed his presence almost right after she walked in, but she really *saw* him now, shrouded in all that misery. Grace blinked, standing still like she was in the woods and had just noticed a bear. Or maybe something more delicate, like a fawn or even a flight of monarch butterflies drying their wings after escaping their cocoons.

"You go practice, Aliyah. We'll talk later." Noah's voice was choked, which made sense. He was on the verge of tears, after all. He and Alex didn't look at each other, both sets of eyes finding something else to fix on as they passed each other in the doorway.

I was about to stop Noah or go after him, I wasn't sure which, but my indecision cost me my choice because Grace rummaged in her dresser, grabbing some compression socks. I shook my head, turned to my own dresser, and got my gym clothes. Our reserve players needed extra practice.

Our tournament was the week after Passover.

Noah and I didn't find time to talk that week. The second-years had standardized tests in the middle of the semester, so he was super busy hitting the books with Elanor. They were in the library, which made it hard to discuss anything emotional. And even though I approached him once, he only told me to be careful and that we'd discuss everything over break.

But that didn't work out so well because Noah wanted to talk to me alone, not with my roommate around. I refused to stop being kind to people who needed it, but sometimes it was damned inconvenient to have a houseguest when your sibling's trying to have a deep and confidential conversation with you.

Grace came home with me on Friday night after class and didn't leave until Tuesday. In the kitchen over breakfast with my family, she said she had to stay in shape and needed time in the gym on campus. But I knew better, because she told me the night before, whispering up from the trundle bed in my room.

She had an appointment with Headmaster Hawkins, the therapy kind. So of course, Izzy and Cadence decided to bring me down to Engine House for pizza. Noah tried to stop me and I almost let him, but I needed a little time out of the house too. At the counter, we grabbed some slices and sodas and hustled into a booth beside the window so we could people watch.

"So, tell me about this boy." Cadence smiled. "The one who took you to the dance."

"Is that what you brought me here for? To go boy crazy?" I raised my eyebrow. I didn't really want to discuss Alex.

"Not exactly. It's just a topic." She shrugged. "Why? What would you rather talk about?"

"How about that Bishop's Row team at Gallows Hill? Let's talk about that instead." I rattled off a string of questions about whether the teams are just limited to changelings or if they'd somehow figured out a way for shifters to channel energy.

"There's not much to tell. I'm not on it." She chuckled. "But we've got a cheer squad. That's what I'm doing."

"So, tell me about cheer squad, then."

"It's not too exciting." She shrugged, then took a bite of her pizza and talked around it. "Mostly, we jump up and down making a lot of noise. The outfits are cute though."

"Don't tell me you're wearing miniskirts with lollipops under them?" Izzy rolled her eyes. One of the things she never liked about the mundane schools we attended earlier in our lives was cheerleading uniforms. She thought them boring and stereotypical, even if the girls wearing them found miniskirts empowering.

"No way." Cadence pulled out her phone, tapping it to fetch a picture. I was totally envious of the fact that cell phones worked at Gallows Hill, but that was beside the point.

The outfit she showed us was something like a jogging suit but covered with sequins. No wonder she loved it. I saw that the squad wasn't just for girls, either.

"That's actually kind of cool." Izzy looked up from the phone. "We've got nothing like that at Messing." She chuckled. "People applaud there by snapping their fingers like a bunch of beatniks."

"But you've got a team, right?" Cadence's eyes widened. "Because your school's going to need it for—"

"Ixnay!" Izzy made a cutting gesture across her throat, reminding me for all the world of a pirate. "Yeah, we do. Nobody who's not on the team admits liking it, though." She snorted. I was getting the impression folks at Izzy's school annoyed her immensely.

"Are you on it?" I realized I sounded like Grace, all questions and no answers, and I got annoyed with her and Dylan for avoiding confrontation. Not a good look, Aliyah.

"I guess." Izzy shrugged. "Shocked everybody I know there, but it's no big deal." Clearly, sports weren't that important to her. But she'd been pretty flat over the whole break. Should I be worried?

Worrying over a psychic? That's a bit beneath you, isn't it? People like them exist for people like us to use as we see fit.

I rolled my eyes at the evil inside voice, but my friends didn't need to know anything about that. Or maybe they did. Could I tell them? I knew I could trust them to keep secrets, but I wasn't sure I should divulge that in a public place like Engine House. Or at all.

Because once again, the voice had a point. Extramagi have a long history of chewing psychics up and spitting them out. And mermaids had gone into hiding ages ago because of them. What if I scared them away and they didn't want to hang out anymore? I wasn't sure I could handle losing the friends I'd known since kindergarten.

"Well, you and Aliyah have something in common, then." Cadence's smile was like sunlight on water.

"Yeah, I know. She's Jane Football, in a manner of speaking." Izzy chuckled at me. "Who knew you'd be a jock?"

"And dating one, too! So, tell us about your boyfriend." Cadence had finished her pizza so she folded her hands, making them flat like a table, then set her chin on them and batted her eyes. That pretty much meant she wouldn't drop the subject of Alex Onassis.

"It sort of happened by accident." I stared at the crumbs on the paper plate in front of me. "Us dating, I mean."

"Like in a rom-com? You spilled coffee on him or something?"

"Not really." I shrugged. "It just sort of happened. I think I'm dating him by default or something because ever since the dance he's just been hanging around with me all the time practically."

"Well, uh. So, what's he like?" Cadence's hand flopped like a fish out of water. Her accompanying laugh was more of a gasp. The conversation was awkward with a side order of cringe sauce.

"Hang on a minute there, Cadence." Izzy shook her head, dropping her pizza crust and placing her hands flat on the table. She meant business. "He's just following you around so you're dating. That sounds majorly unhealthy."

"I don't know from healthy." I sighed, shaking my head like my body couldn't decide which emotion to show. "I've never had a boyfriend before, so I don't know what normal is."

"Let me ask you something." Izzy narrowed her eyes. "It's extra personal, so I hope you don't mind."

"Personal's what I expect from my best friends. Right?" I was worried that the worst was happening. Were we growing apart? "Go ahead."

"Okay, so Logan Pierce took you to the Parents' Night dance." She tilted her head, brown hair cascading over one shoulder. "And you didn't end up dating *him* by default, right? Why not?"

"Because Logan and I talked about it." My breath caught in my throat because, like any psychic worth her salt, she'd led me to a conclusion. "We agreed both of us feel totally platonic about each other. Like good friends, and we're happy like that."

"So how come you're default-dating this Alex guy when I assume he didn't bother discussing your feelings on the matter?" Her nostrils flared.

"Wow." I struggled to swallow past the lump in my throat. "Time's just kind of gotten away from me. There's some pretty serious stuff going on with friends at school, like potentially life-threatening."

"Oh, my God, Aliyah, I'm sorry." Cadence leaned back, blinking. "If I'd known, I never would've kept bugging you about this whole Alex thing."

"No, it's a good thing you brought it up, Cadence." Izzy nodded. "Because Aliyah definitely needs to stop and think about whether she even wants to date this dude."

"Yeah, you're right." Cadence sighed. "So, tell us about your other friends, then."

"Okay." I took a deep breath and leaned forward so I could lower my voice and keep name-dropping to a minimum. Medical information was private. "You remember Hal Hawkins?"

They nodded. After that, I launched into a brief timeline of his health's deterioration, what Hal had told me, and my theories. Cadence chewed the inside of her cheek, a common habit when she was deeply worried. But Izzy went pale, which did not bode well. Not at all.

I told you he was dying, but did you listen?

"He's felt too sick to leave campus. Class takes a lot out of him even when he takes it easy." I sighed. "But when Grace went to campus this morning, I asked her to track him down and see if he'll come over tomorrow. And bring him to Bubbe's office."

"Why?" Cadence blinked. "What's an extraveterinarian going to do for a magus?"

"A blood test on a separate record from the ones his family controls, for one thing."

"Is that legal?" Cadence pursed her lips. "He's a minor, right?"

Izzy turned her head, staring in shock at Cadence. Thinking of the law was not usually her wheelhouse.

"I don't know, but at this point, I hardly care." My hands curled into fists. I was prepared to fight for my friend's life, legalities be damned.

Izzy stood so suddenly she knocked her chair over. The entire staff and all the customers stared. Everyone saw her pointing at me with one hand while rummaging in her bag of cards with the other. And when she slapped the omen down on the table between us, I had nothing at all to say about it.

For once, an intelligent choice.

It was the nine of swords. Izzy has been reading cards around me since before she could read words, so I was fully aware of what this one meant. Guilt, plain and simple. Secrets that kept you up at night, weights on your mind and heart that you couldn't shake.

But it got worse. Not because of the card, but because Izzy sometimes channeled coincidence. It was all part of being a precognitive psychic who saw the future with the aid of items instead of in dreams or through scrying. She was about to unleash a major truth on me right here in the middle of my favorite restaurant.

No pressure. Who am I kidding? It was like being at the bottom of the sea.

"You must cast off your burdens or sink with them. The time is sooner than you imagine, and You. Are. Not. Prepared."

Izzy collapsed backward, which meant she'd fall. Her chair was on the floor, legs stretching and threatening like the swords on that card. She could seriously injure herself on it.

"Ember, go!"

My dragonet launched herself off my shoulder, swooping down toward Izzy to grab her by the shoulders of her cardigan. Golden talons punched holes through knit fabric, which held, thank goodness. But a critter no bigger than a small cat couldn't hope to keep a swooning psychic upright for long.

Cadence and I stood, but we were on the other side of the table. We were too late. Fortunately, the person at the table behind her turned and rose to the occasion. More like he raised the chair.

With magic.

It was Lee Young, from Hawthorn. I knew he'd be staying in Salem this week, but I had no idea he loved this pizza place as much as we did. His wood magic easily affected the fallen seat, since aside from the screws, it was entirely made from his element.

The chair slid into place behind Izzy just in time to catch her as Ember lost her grip. Lee stood and moved to the empty seat beside Izzy. He reached for her soda cup and placed it in front of her, then opened his coat and let Scratch out.

"Make sure she's okay, then we'll try reviving her."

Cadence nodded. This looked like familiar territory for both of them, which had me totally stumped. Clearly, Lee had become well acquainted with both of my friends from town. Which was good, all things considered. Nobody else I know could've pulled off that rescue stunt.

Ember returned to my shoulder as Scratch climbed into Izzy's lap. The Sumxu stood on her hind legs, peering at Izzy's face and tilting her head from one side to the other. Her voice was squeaky with a lilt at the end like she asked a series of questions. Scratch sounded for all the world like an inquisitive guinea pig, even though she was a magical lop-eared cat.

Now that things were relatively calm, the other bystanders turned away and went about the business of enjoying their pizza. I stuck around, watching Lee do his thing. It was clear he was planning to go into some sort of extrahuman medicine in the future. Wood magi often did.

I wondered if maybe I should let him in on Hal's problem, but that wasn't for me to decide. Izzy came out of it in half a minute, immediately thirsty. I wondered how Lee had expected that. Maybe she'd done readings for him before or something, but if she'd channeled coincidence while doing it, it must've been a heavy topic.

She sucked down soda, grabbing the nine of swords off the table and putting it away in her bag. She looked up at me, saying nothing. I nodded, understanding. This was just part of her being psychic.

Cadence and I decided to cut things short, packing up Izzy's pizza and helping her out the door. Lee came along and walked all the way to Izzy's house with us. Once we handed her off to Abuela, Lee nodded and waved, heading back toward campus.

Cadence lingered for moment, so I asked if she was all right.

"I've been better, honestly. Sorry for acting so weird. But there's a lot going on I can't talk about. You probably don't understand."

"No, I get it." I reached out, patted her shoulder. "Hey, I'm the one who got the nine of swords, remember?"

"I thought I did." Cadence blinked.

I stood there musing. Izzy pointed across the table, where Cadence and I both sat. It could have been either of us. "Or maybe both."

"Both what?" Cadence chuckled softly. "Your inside voice is out of control again, huh?"

"I guess. I never could quite get a handle on that." I sighed. "It's gotten me into all sorts of trouble lately."

"I'm sorry about Alex. All the pushing I did, the assumptions I made." She held out her arms. "Can you forgive me?"

"Always." I hugged my friend, realizing that we were going to have loads to catch up on over the summer. But right now, standing out in the rapidly chilling air of late afternoon, wasn't the time. "Listen, Cadence. I'll definitely see you again this week. Hang in there. I've got to talk to Noah; it's overdue and important, and there's something I need to do before I can really figure the whole Alex thing out."

"Okay." She nodded. "Don't be a stranger. It feels like ages since you used the orb. Don't forget about us while you're in school. We all need each other, always have."

"I won't. I promise."

I walked up the driveway, glancing up at the living room window. Noah sat in it, watching me approach the house. My parent's car was not there, so we'd finally have time.

CHAPTER ELEVEN

Upstairs in Noah's room, we sat at the foot of his bed, our hands curled around mugs of hot chocolate. His had whipped cream with sprinkles and mine, marshmallows. But otherwise, we were practically mirror images of each other.

"This chocolate is forbidden." I smirked. "In your room."

"I can't risk Mom and Dad walking in. Or anyone else, for that matter." Noah shook his head as though he wore a ten-ton crown.

"You can't even talk about this in front of Bubbe?" Our grandmother was always more accepting than Mom and Dad. She could afford it, because our discipline wasn't in her hands.

"No. Well, I mean, I could." Noah stared at the ceiling, searching for words. "I'd trust her with that, I mean. But this is all just too painful."

"I understand."

"You can't possibly." He gazed down at his nearly melted whipped cream. "You've never been in love." Lotan slithered down the bed toward Noah, twining around his forearm, a gesture of support.

"Is that what this is about?" I was totally confused, and not just because I'd never been in romantic love with anyone. "Were you in love with Alex?"

"No, never." Noah's nose wrinkled like that time a skunk got into the backyard. "I caught him and Darren. You know, in the act? It was the day we got back to campus. Alex said some pretty awful stuff when I walked in there, like how he knew Darren had a boyfriend and didn't care. That was why we broke up."

"Holy shit, Noah." I spoke the oath so softly, it was barely there.

"Did he even tell you he was bi?" Noah's lips pressed together, paling. "Risky stuff, not talking about that sort of thing after dating for this long."

"I should have figured." I shook my head. "I mean, he asked if I was asexual. I totally don't know, and now I'm all confused."

"Maybe he's right." Noah shrugged. "But you know what they say about broken clocks twice a day, so that's why he's no good. Why you should dump him."

"I get it. Alex hurt you and Darren, and you don't want him to hurt me too."

"Pretty much." Noah closed his eyes, holding the hot chocolate under his nose. I did the same.

There's just something about chocolate. Even if you don't have a major sweet tooth and prefer it salted or spicy like Izzy, it helps. If there was anything on this Earth totally comforting and benign, it was chocolate in any way, shape, or form.

"I'm not even sure how we started going out. I went over it today with Izzy and Cadence."

"What did they have to say?"

Only last year, Noah would've snorted, skeptical that my friends could possibly give me any useful input on romance. But he understood that seven months at a specialized high school changed a person.

"That it sounds pretty toxic, actually. I'm only with him because he won't leave me alone. It's like default mode, you know?"

"No, I don't know. Because I've never been with someone just for the heck of it." He tilted his head, dark hair falling over one side of his face. "I won't date a guy unless I'm totally into him, whether that's because he's hot or fun or smart. Or even all three, like Darren."

"I'm not sure I've ever felt like that about anybody." I shook my head, immediately rescinding my lie before the evil inside voice butted in. "No. There's exactly one person."

"But he's taken, isn't he?" He raised an eyebrow. "You don't have to say his name."

"That's the size and shape of it, Noah." I leaned against his bedpost. Ember hopped off the dresser, gliding down to settle in my lap. "I'm doomed."

"No, you're not. One of the things Elanor kept telling me since the breakup was that they call it first love for a reason. It's the exact opposite of last love, right?"

"That's awfully deep stuff coming from her." I shrugged. "Logan always talks about how shallow she is."

"It's an act because that's what their parents want." Noah sipped his chocolate. "Logan never got with that program and he suffers for it every day."

"I know. I'm his friend remember?" I sighed. "Why do they make it so hard? His parents, I mean. And Faith's are even worse, encouraging their kids to terrorize each other. Why are they so horrible to their kids?" I drank some chocolate because it was the only thing I thought might ease my anguish.

"I don't think there's any particular reason, Aliyah." Noah leaned against his bedpost, taking a long sip of his now-temperate beverage. "Maybe we're just extremely lucky in the parental unit department."

"I love them so much. How do you deal with missing them at school? You don't come home very often, and I never understand why."

"That's exactly why I don't. If I did, it'd be like ripping off a band-aid every single time and I'd never heal."

Even growing up under the same roof and only a year apart, we were practically opposite—another mystery in the familial department. I was unsure of what to say about that, so I changed the subject.

"Will you ever forgive Darren?"

"Oh, Aliyah. I already did, months ago. Moments after I found out it happened, in fact."

"I don't understand." There was an awful lot of that going around for me today. "Why aren't you back together, then?"

"Darren doesn't want that. He's not in love with me." He sniffled, tears welling up even after all that time. "Said he never was."

"Oh, Noah. I'm so sorry." I set the hot chocolate down and open my arms, reaching toward my brother. Ember moved out of my lap, peeping softly.

He put his down too, with Lotan curled around the ceramic, and we hugged. As we sat, rocking back and forth in time to the tears falling on my shoulder, I realized something.

Noah had been carrying all this hurt secretly, hiding it under a veneer of cattiness and social climbing. That was why he'd followed Charity last semester, becoming one of her most tenacious hangers-on. While I set fires, he'd upended his social life. So much of it made sense now. And so did one other thing, from this new perspective.

If Noah was this traumatized about Alex, Darren, and my default dating status, what would it do to him when he found out I was an extramagus?

He'll probably die of a broken heart. Or kill you.

I started crying too because that was the only possible response for the evil inside voice this time. Our combined weeping made a melancholy sort of music that filled the room, heavier than the air we breathed.

By the time we finished, the chocolate was tepid. We didn't mind. I sat with my brother in silence, finishing our illicit upstairs beverages. When the cups were empty, we headed back to the kitchen together. For now.

Dinner was at five-thirty that night. Grace was back in time and told me Hal was coming at eight for Nin to have an extraveterinarian visit, so after dinner, Grace and I headed out to meet Hal on Essex Street.

The door to Hawthorn Academy was right next to the Witch's Brew this time, so we got ourselves some Red Zinger tea and an extra for Hal. When he emerged alone, we were both ready. Grace and I both rushed over to the door because he was awfully teetery on the cobblestones.

"Thanks." His smile was dim tonight, which really said something because Hal Hawkins usually had the brightest smile of anyone I knew.

"We're just going to take a nice, slow stroll here." Grace linked an arm through Hal's. "Like we're a bunch of tourist looky-loos, okay?"

"That sounds great." Hal nodded.

Nin poked her head out of his jacket's collar, squeaking at Ember. She glanced down at Lune and flared her nostrils in greeting.

She didn't look so great either, but mostly in ways that made me think the little Pharaoh's Rat hadn't slept well. Totally understandable. When a magus bonded to a familiar got sick, the poor critter ended up dropping the ball big time on their self-care.

We made it all the way to Izzy's house before Hal needed to rest, which meant this was a better day than I thought for him. The break from classes must have given him some much-needed time off from using his magic. We sat on the front stoop outside the psychic shop, drinking our tea.

Izzy waved from the window, then held up a feather duster. Clearly, Abuela had given her some evening chores, probably because she wasn't around much during the day. At least she looked like she'd recovered from that intense soothsaying at lunch.

The cups were empty by the time Hal was ready to get back up again. We easily made the walk between numbers 10 and 11 and up the drive to 10-1/2. Instead of opening the door to the stairs that led to my apartment, I reached for the shop's latch. Bubbe was expecting us.

"Come along back now." The corners of my grandmother's lips turned up, although I knew for sure she wasn't really smiling. Hal's appearance must've really shaken her. The fact that this was a good day for him made me feel horrible about waiting this long to get him here.

She brought us right into the kitchen and let Hal sit at the table.

Nin jumped out of his coat and scuttled around for a bit on the blue and white linoleum.

"Yes, little one." She nodded at the Pharaoh's Rat. "We're all concerned."

"You can't understand her, can you?" Hal tilted his head.

"No, but it's obvious from her body language that she's deeply worried about you." Bubbe opened a cabinet and brought out a blood exam kit.

The kits were in boxes wrapped in blue fabric. They contained one of the blood tests I mentioned before that we'd be using on Hal, and also a set of instruments for examining the ears, noses, and throats of most familiars. These had lights and magnifiers on them.

There was also a bisected basin, designed to either take samples or provide food and water. Because Bubbe was not really doing an exam on Nin today, she dumped a handful of treats in one side and poured water in the other. After that, she placed it in front of the little critter.

"Peep?" Ember headbutted me on the cheek, then looked at Nin and Lune.

"In a minute, girl. Let her eat first."

When Nin was done, Ember joined her on the floor, but the Pharaoh's Rat was near exhaustion. Ember escorted her across the floor toward a corner near the radiator. Lune had already parked his tail there, but he made room. Nin settled down between the moon hare and the dragonet, and Ember put her wing over the lot of them.

"Thank goodness for friends." Hal grinned.

"Indeed." Bubbe had already pricked his finger and was smearing blood on the plate for the test. She looked up at the clock to check the time, then down at the sample again.

We waited a full minute before the plate changed color, going purple. I had no idea what that meant, but Bubbe didn't like it one bit.

"How long have you had your powers, Hal?"

"To the point I could use them for anything besides feeling magic energy? Less than a year."

"What about before that?"

"Oh. Almost three."

"And your mother's not a magus?"

"No. She's psychic."

"And that's all?"

"Yeah. Psychometry. Touching things and getting an impression."

"I see. And do her powers always work?"

"You know, I never thought about that. Give me a minute." Hal closed his eyes. And yes, it was close to a minute before he opened them again and gave us an answer. "No, not always. I remember she had a problem a few years back at Gallows Hill. She couldn't tell which student had vandalized the lockers, and the principal pulled her yellow slip. She almost got accused of lying about her status."

He meant the license all practicing psychics have, especially when they worked in institutions like law enforcement or education.

"There's one more thing I need to test, Hal. Is that okay with you?"

"Sure. I'm just so tired of not knowing what's wrong with me." His eyes looked dry, like they were cried out and had given up on making any more tears over this mystery illness.

"Just a moment." Bubbe left the room, heading down to the end of the hall where the supply closet was.

While we waited, I puttered around the kitchen, cleaning the basin now that Nin was done with it. I just couldn't sit still, this was so nerve-racking. Bubbe had definitely found something. Whatever it was, it was serious enough that she wanted more information.

She came back with a venipuncture kit and a vial with a serial number on the name section of the label. An anonymous test of some kind.

"I never knew you had these kinds of human supplies here." I almost dropped the basin I was drying.

"Up until now, you haven't needed to." She unwrapped the needle with its tubing apparatus, leaving the business end capped. "When you get into the business of helping familiars, creatures so closely bonded to other beings, you find yourself crossing the line once in a while. And while I'm not licensed to treat illnesses of extrahumans, I can certainly send samples out so they can seek the care they need from properly qualified professionals."

"You mean we'll have to wait for the results?" Hal watched her swab the inside of his elbow with alcohol.

"Not all of them, but let me get the sample ready first. The holidays are coming, and the night courier will be here in minutes. I don't want to miss this window of opportunity."

She deftly punctured Hal's vein and pushed the rubber stopper on the vial onto the spike. Blood fountained into it. When she was done, she asked me to put pressure on the wound and bandage it, then hurried out the door and toward the front.

As I taped up Hal's tiny injury, I heard her speaking to someone out there, probably the courier. When she returned, he was all bandaged.

"I want you to listen to me very carefully, young Master Hawkins. Aliyah, you and Grace ought to head down to the storeroom and fetch some multivitamins for Nin. We don't want him returning to campus empty-handed."

Grace stood, and I tossed the bandage wrapper in the trash. We didn't hesitate to follow her instructions because we knew Bubbe would do the right thing by our friend, except Hal didn't want privacy.

"I don't want to hear this alone if it's all the same to you, Dr. Morgenstern."

"It's your right to privacy were talking about here."

"I trust my friends with my life." His smile was faint but present. "They brought me to you in the first place."

I blinked, almost sagging against the wall. I could hardly believe what I was hearing. Even though he knew beyond a doubt that I was an extramagus, Harold Hawkins trusted me implicitly. Grace took things in stride much more easily than I did. She had an admirable handle on this situation.

We grabbed chairs, dragging them around to his side of the table so we could sit next to him. Once we were all set, Bubbe nodded.

"The sample I sent off will verify the reason for this, but the test I did right here in this room is practically infallible." She reached across the table, taking both of Hal's hands in her own. She held them gently, as though they were made of eyelash-thin blown glass.

"You mean the purple smear?" He nodded. "Okay, what's it mean?"

"You have pernicious magiglobular anemia, a rare disease without any true cure." She gazed at his hands. "Symptoms include difficulty conjuring magical energy, inability to absorb magic energy from this realm's environment, and extreme fatigue after engaging in magical activity. Therapies include direct infusions from magical wells in the Under, which is easily done on campus. Doctor Br—I mean, Zeke has centuries of experience with those."

"I'm getting them every day. Sometimes more than once." He sighed, flexing his fingers slightly. "But I'm on the Bishop's Row team. That must be why it's so bad right now."

"When your test comes back, either visit me or find a way that we can chat. I've got a few other ideas, the basis for things that researchers in Boston are working with. Palliative, for comfort measures, these are. And I believe you may be in a position to give one of them a try on your own."

"Thanks, Dr. Morgenstern."

"That's not all, young man." Bubbe looked him right in the eye. "You should not continue with Bishop's Row."

"But Doc, we've got a tournament starting on Monday night. All our strategies hang on my space magic. I can't sit it out."

"You participate at extreme risk. Your results will be back Monday morning, so if the alternative therapy I mentioned will work for you, there's time to try it before your game. It won't make playing risk-free, but your energy levels won't crash as easily for a few hours afterward. However, you'll sit out on Tuesday if my hunch is correct. You'll sleep the clock round. But it will give your team time for alternate strategies after you stop playing."

"If you don't mind my asking, what's your hunch?" Hal pulled his hands back, staring at the backs of them, at the veins standing out.

"There are other forms of magiglobular anemia. They're generally caused by diet or environment, and people with those live full lives using magipsychic medicine every day. But the pernicious kind is genetic, and those treatments don't work. The only possible way you can have it is if someone in your family tree is a Dampyr."

"I understand." Whatever conclusion Hal came to, he didn't share it, at least for now. The pressure was on for my friend.

"Do you have any other questions?"

"No. I'll be sure to get in contact somehow, although short of leaving campus, I'm not sure."

Oh, dear. There's nothing to be done. All this effort for nothing.

I closed my eyes and clenched my fists, deciding how to defy the evil inside voice this time—and there was only one way. Because there was something to be done, but it meant revealing one of my secrets. A tame one, thankfully.

"I've got a communication orb at school." I opened my eyes, gazing right into Bubbe's. "I'll arrange for Hal to use it sometime Monday afternoon."

"Excellent." My grandmother's smile warmed my heart.

"You could get expelled for that." Hal blinked. "Not that I'm going to tell anyone at this point, but wow. Thanks, Aliyah, you're saving my life here."

"She has a way of doing that." Grace put her arm around Hal, patting his shoulder. "Saving the world one magus at a time."

They looked at me, grinning; they got me. I couldn't protest or go on about how I was doomed to go mad and turn evil someday because of what I was, not in front of my grandmother. And they knew it. Maybe this was their attempt to save *me*.

"I've got to feed the animals and close up for Passover, so unless you young folks want to clean some litter boxes—"

"No, we're good." I stood, assisting Hal to his feet, along with Grace. The last thing I wanted was for him to insist on doing chores while he was this exhausted.

"Thanks again, Dr. Morgenstern."

"I'd tell you not to mention it, but..." She rummaged in a pocket, produced a bottle of vitamins formulated for small magical carnivores, and passed them to Hal. "Give her one per day with food."

Hal nodded, then beckoned to Nin, who came scuttling across the floor. There must've been vitamins in the treats Bubbe gave her because she looked better already. Lune and Ember followed, both stretching before coming along after us.

For the matter of that, Hal looked better too. A diagnosis can have that effect right after it's made. I'd seen it a million times in here when magi discovered what conditions their familiars had, even a few of the terminal ones. Knowledge was power, even when the only control you had was how to face death.

We headed down the hall, through the waiting room, and out the door. We took our time again strolling down Essex Street, steeped in the remains of the evening.

CHAPTER TWELVE

Passover was the celebration of liberation, but I felt like a slave to my powers. And also to the evil inside voice, because it hadn't left me alone for a whole day the entire semester. Its constant presence, naysaying half my choices and putting down everything from my academics to friendships, was an albatross around my neck.

I wished there was a way to be free of it, but the problem with maladies of the mind was that you couldn't get away. There was no running from a bully inside your head. Even with distraction, there was always part of your brain working without your knowledge. Mine tended to run counter to what was healthy.

When we'd celebrated Yom Kippur, the weight of my stress had lifted, something I'd experienced before. But with Passover, it was all about appreciating the freedoms you had while remembering what it was like to live without them. The Seder plate literally symbolized fight and flight from oppression.

All I could see was the prison of lies I'd built for myself. I barely remembered what it was like anymore, being open with my family. My mind had slipped, and my heart was just as bad. I knew what I wished to be free of, but it was utterly impossible to break those chains. I'd never heard of anyone losing their extramagus powers.

So, because I couldn't cast off my solar magic, visit plagues upon it, or part a sea to drown it, the only possible course was confessing everything. Being honest had always been my fallback until this year. The yoke of dishonesty galled me, wearing holes in my resolve and fraying the fabric of all my relationships.

At least I wasn't going it completely alone, although I'd always wonder whether my school friends only accepted me because I kept their secrets. Despite that, it was a comfort that Grace knew and was with me that day as we prepared for our Seder. Bubbe baked downstairs, so I was in the upstairs kitchen with Noah and Grace, helping Mom and Dad with everything else. This included finishing the soup, roast, and brussels sprouts, but also making sure we'd gotten rid of all the leavened grains in the house.

"Are you really throwing this out?" Grace raised an eyebrow as she held up a bag of Bubbe's challah rolls.

"If you want to bring it back to school with you, go ahead. Just stow it in your luggage because we can't keep it in the kitchen." My mother nodded toward the stairs.

"Thanks. I've been craving this bread since Thanksgiving." Grace dashed up the stairs and returned in a few moments.

That was it for leftover leavened goods. Tonight, and for the next eight days, it'd be all matzoh all the time. Fortunately, there were several varieties, so there was plenty to bring back to school, and I wouldn't get bored with it.

During my long-overdue conversations yesterday, Mom and Dad had gone out to get the symbolic foods and all the special Kosher for Passover stuff they'd use this week. The most well-known was matzoh, but there were so many others.

From pasta to jam and everything in between, there was a version that was Kosher for Passover. That seemed sort of extra, but it was all because the ancient Israelites didn't have time to let their bread rise as they fled Egypt. Things like meats are specially blessed by a rabbi, but other more shelf-stable foods had substitutions for any leavened ingredient, and those got certified too. Nothing like croutons or breadcrumbs were in those items. Yes, we got that particular about it.

Most of the work was already done. All that needed doing now was setting the table. It was different from Thanksgiving because Passover had both religious and cultural significance. You didn't just yeet thousands of years of tradition without a good reason, so this night was different from any others.

One way was in how we arranged our seating. We sat upright at all our other meals, but on Passover, we got comfy. The *Haggadah*, that book of instructions for Passover, called it reclining. What that really meant was we could put our feet up or lean back or add extra cushions to the chairs. One year, Noah even set up piles of pillows on the floor, insisting he and I have our meal there.

We set up the Seder plate. This was the big symbol energy of the entire holiday, so it always went right in the center of the table. Ours was enameled wood, white with blue edging, with four sections ringing the sides and one in the middle. Remember when I said before that this holiday symbolizes escape from slavery in Egypt? Every item on that plate represented a different part of what our ancient forebears experienced.

I helped Mom put everything on it, just like last year. The only thing different this time was Grace watching over my shoulder. And Ember, perched on top of the refrigerator.

"What's that parsley in middle?" Grace asked.

"*Karpas*." Mom added more. "It represents how the Israelites first came to Egypt. Joseph brought them."

"Who?"

"You know." I snapped my fingers. "Remember that musical we watched last week with the guy in the coat of many colors who interprets dreams? And for a while, it was good. Sort of like parsley when you first taste it."

"Raw parsley doesn't have a pleasant aftertaste." She wrinkled her nose.

"That's why we use it," Dad said. "Life in ancient Egypt was like that. Bitter later on. At one point, we'll dip it in saltwater because it got so bad."

"That actually looks good." Grace pointed as the paste of fruit and nuts. "What is it?"

"*Haroset.*" I spooned some on the appropriate section of the plate. "This is my favorite because it's delicious."

"What does it mean?"

"It's all about the labor," Noah answered. "The mortar we used, building for the Pharaoh. But this stuff's nasty." He wrinkled his nose and dropped a dollop of horseradish on the plate. "*Maror*, standing in for the bitterness of slavery."

"I knew people who had it with sandwiches on the regular." Grace shrugged. "But yeah, it's strong. Do you actually eat any of this stuff?"

This time, Bubbe answered.

"At one point during the meal, we mix the *haroset* with *maror*, because while labor can be sweet, forced labor is bitter. It gets pressed between two pieces of matzoh, just like mortar between bricks. And we eat the *karpas*, both before the saltwater dip and after. But two items on that plate, we don't eat. They're for contemplation."

"Right." I nodded. "The *zeroah* and *beitzah*."

"The what and the who now?" Grace blinked.

"*Zeroah* is that lamb shank," Dad explained. "It symbolizes the Israelite's sacrifices and celebrations after reaching Jerusalem. And *beitzah* is this roasted egg. Any guesses on what it means, Grace?"

"Life and hope?"

"Egg-zactly." Dad chuckled.

Everyone groaned.

"But there's a little more than that to Passover." Bubbe patted my shoulder. "The egg reminds us that this too shall pass."

For me this year, that was an enormous truth, one so big that perhaps I hadn't been able to see it through all my inner turmoil and chaos.

The plate was finally done, so we brought it out and set it on the table. Noah followed with three pieces of matzoh covered in a cloth. Dad brought out the dish with saltwater for the parsley.

Noah headed back to the kitchen, then returned with an orange. This was something he did last year after coming out because an orange symbolized the social and emotional fruitfulness that comes with including everyone in our society. He set it on his right beside his plate, which was where we always put the items that represented liberation to us personally.

Grace had some of that shimmery copper fabric, the stuff that had been the overlay on her dress for Valentine's Day. Making her own clothes, stuff that rivaled a masterwork of tailoring, was an amazing accomplishment.

Bubbe had a carefully preserved photo of her father as a boy, standing in Trafalgar Square in London. He'd just arrived there as part of the Kindertransport program, rescued from certain death in Nazi camps.

Dad and Mom usually placed their wedding rings there because they always told us they'd saved each other, though never how. But this year, it was different. Dad had his diploma from Hawthorn Academy. I think because both Noah and I attended, working hard at school, he wanted to show us how important education was to living a free life.

Mom had a clipping from the Providence Journal. It showed a picture of her, one I never knew existed. She walked down the steps in front of the Extrahuman Courthouse downtown, cameras and microphones pointed at her face. She wasn't looking down, although the shot they chose for this piece was in profile. My mother faced whichever reporter or photographer stood in front of her, staring them down with a gaze as intimidating as any eagle's. The date was over the summer, only one week before she gave me the swimsuit.

The headline read *Estranged Hopewell sister testifies against extramagus brother.*

I felt strange that I didn't have something of my own this year. Usually, it was some paper or project from school I had done particularly well on, or something from Izzy or Cadence, symbolizing how important friendship is. But I had nothing this year because I felt caged.

Our readings came from the abbreviated *Haggadah*, which didn't take long. This was good because my stomach already grumbled, and

Grace was in the same boat. We'd skipped lunch. Big mistake, but easily rectified.

My father recited the Plagues of Egypt in Hebrew, something he'd always done. After that came the Four Questions, which Noah and I took turns reciting. Reading them wasn't required because they were in our memories forever now. It was something we did together every Passover. Usually, it's the youngest child, but being only a year apart meant he only would have read them once in his life.

One of the best things about this part of Seder was that when we had guests, like Grace this year or Izzy and Cadence on others, they got to learn why everything was just so on Passover. Grace didn't even have to ask why this night was different, why we ate only matzoh and no bread, why we dipped bitter herbs twice, and why we got cozy seats.

The short answers were that we celebrated freedom, the Israelites had no time to let the bread rise, we needed to remember bitterness to appreciate sweetness, remembering tears helps us appreciate joy, and people needed time and space to rest and celebrate after going through trauma.

So that was Passover in a nutshell, but my dilemma was far from over. I had nothing to share because I felt hollow, as though I was the *beitzah* egg but just the shell. I sat staring at it, sometimes averting my gaze to the news clipping at Mom's right.

Bubbe's story about her photograph was part of family legend. Noah's explanation for his orange was the same as last year. Dad's was new but predictable. Grace said only one sentence, that with freedom comes responsibility to craft a life from what you've learned.

We all hung on Mom's every word. This was a story even Dad might not have heard in full. She'd offered to testify, wasn't responding to subpoena. She said it was her duty to go on record as saying that Richard's crimes were part of a lifelong pattern. That he'd never change or get better unless he admitted to his shortcomings and sought help on his own.

How could I be the daughter of woman this brave? One who summoned the courage to leave her oppressive family, then decades later, spoke out against the worst and most dangerous of them? And she had done it all without a familiar; that was something I got from Dad's side of the family, not hers. The Hopewells were nothing if not supremacists, in more ways than one. They believed magi were above all other people and that magic creatures were there for our amusement, not as friends or even companions.

I wasn't sure how she bucked the odds, but as I stared again at the *beitzah* egg, contemplating that the one constant in this world was change, I felt something tiny but warm, like that first ray of sunlight hitting the icicle that forms every year outside my window. The one that brings it down, eventually.

Maybe I wasn't brave like Mom because that was not what I needed to overcome my circumstances. Maybe I needed my family and friends. Perhaps the best way to fight my inevitable descent into the madness too much magic brought was just love.

"Ember, come here, girl." I patted the empty space to my right, where my item would be. No material thing I possessed could represent this new faint hope for redemption.

"What's this, Aliyah?" Bubbe raised an eyebrow.

"This year, it's my bond with Ember that liberates me." I managed a grin as she swooped toward me.

As my dragonet lit on the table between my brother and me, I understood that the lies needed to stop, but not tonight. I'd keep my secret until after the game tomorrow because just like Hal, I'd let down our entire year if I had to bow out. All I had to do was make sure I didn't accidentally conjure anything solar during the game.

Piece of cake, right?

CHAPTER THIRTEEN

On Monday, we were all back at school, finally. Faith didn't get in until the last train up from Boston on Sunday. Logan's flight was a red-eye, so he didn't arrive until early in the morning. He practically fell asleep in his eggs, so it was a good thing he wasn't on the team.

Alex kept his distance. Instead of following me closely as he'd done since the dance, he had his head down over his books and notes. Maybe he was behind on studying, or perhaps Ember made faces at him when I wasn't looking. More likely, he knew I'd spent the whole week in the same house as Noah.

The plan was to have a chat with him later today. For all I knew, he'd been as weighed down by guilt this year as I was. Or maybe not. The biggest takeaway I had this Passover came from Mom and also what she'd testified about Uncle Richard. Some people wanted to do better. Others weren't ready. If Alex was, maybe that'd help me decide how I felt about him.

We had a half-day of classes, which was the case all week because of the tournament. So, we went to homeroom and then Creatives, where we could all chat before heading to the locker room. Alex sat at a drafting table, sketching something. All my other friends hovered over a table in the middle, making collages.

"Aliyah, what's wrong with you?" Faith shook her head. "You've been stiff all day, almost awkward. I saw you drop your pencil like twenty times in homeroom. Are you nervous about the game?"

"No. She's carrying something important for me." Hal glanced at my knapsack, which looked heavier than usual.

It wasn't. I just put extra padding in there to protect the communication orb. Izzy had brought hers to Bubbe's office before leaving for school, so she could take Hal's call.

"Okay." Faith put her hands on her hips, tapping her toe and giving her boyfriend side-eye. "This is something to do with that stuff we talked about last night, right?"

"Yes."

I knew what the alternative therapy was, too, because Bubbe had let me in on it. She'd even given me a clinical description so they could try it before the game. Yes, I was going to use my contraband orb that could get me expelled right there in the locker room before a tournament game.

Grace had an idea on how to do that covertly. She offered to hide the orb and Bubbe's side of the conversation from casual view with umbral magic. Anyone walking by would see Hal but would think he held a more benign item. He'd be talking to it, so we'd need to cover his voice mundanely. This meant we'd need to shut him in the sauna without turning it on or sit in one of the showers with the water running.

We all agreed that the sauna was the better choice. It was a gender-neutral area, while two of the showers weren't. The entrance to the one gender-neutral shower we had was in a high-traffic area, while the sauna was off in the corner. Also, nobody used saunas before a workout, but sometimes folks showered before games to invigorate themselves.

We bailed on Creatives early, heading to the locker room. The headmaster let us go because it was our first real game. He must have assumed we were super nervous and wanted to be totally prepared, which worked in our favor. Hopefully, more than this would go right today, but I wasn't counting any chickens.

The wood-lined room was dry and warm; quiet, too. I bet the Night Creatures would have loved to use it as a studio if it weren't for the fire pit in the corner that supplied the extreme heat when the sauna was in use. Hal sat on a bench, and I got the orb out of my knapsack. Grace touched it, conjuring her magic to obscure its true nature. Once I set it in Hal's hands, the orb resembled a library book, at least unless you got closer than arm's length.

It would seem weird if anyone walked in. I mean, who read books in the sauna, especially when it wasn't even on. I figured other students might imagine this was a weird sports-related superstition. Coach Pickman would not be so easily fooled, so I positioned myself by the window as a lookout.

"Hello?" Bubbe's voice was tinny coming through the orb. "Am I speaking with Harold?

"Hi, Dr. Morgenstern," Hal replied quietly, nodding.

"Well, your results came back, and you definitely have Dampyr DNA. It's a significant amount too, so that means it's a very close family member."

"So it's my mom." Hal's voice was flat.

"Perhaps, but the only way to know for certain is if your parents take their own tests."

"Well, at least this can't make Easter dinner awkward since that already happened." Hal's words belied the gravity in his tone.

Getting hit with a secret identity out of left field was like being in a car crash. Everything slowed down. Each object in your field of vision was at an impossible angle, and when you tried to make sense of things, they moved again. There was nothing about the world that you could pin down in an immediate sense. The only thing that helped after it all stopped was time and distance. "And Hal doesn't have much of either."

"I don't have what now?" Hal blinked.

"Sorry." I shook my head. "Inside voice being a jerk."

Oh, you don't know the half of it.

I closed my eyes, leaning against the door, using my ears instead for my lookout duties. It was hard to focus on whether there were footsteps outside the sauna, though, not with Hal getting bleak for the first time where his friends could see it. I wouldn't lie to myself and pretend someone as ill as Hal hadn't despaired in private.

"Is there a way for me to find out if my dad's really my father?"

"I'd say he is. You resemble him quite closely when he was your age, in feature and build. Besides, space magic is quite rare. It's practically impossible that if your mother were unfaithful, she'd have found another space magus to carry on with on this side of the Atlantic."

"Nothing's impossible for magi." Hal's voice cracked. He cleared his throat and continued, "Pardon my language, but coincidence is a bitch, Dr. Morgenstern."

"I already checked the registry, Harold. There are no space magi besides you and your father on this side of the Atlantic Ocean. And you're pardoned in my book."

"That means nothing. Mom's on the registry as a psychic, not a Dampyr. There must be something more to this than even you found out. How do I look for it?" He sniffled. "You're the only person who's given me anything like a real answer about any of this, so what do I do now?"

"You try the therapy. You play your game." Bubbe's voice was too even, the way it got when she delivered the worst news about a patient.

"I'm talking about in the long-term, doctor."

"Get through this day. Come by anytime this week. We'll discuss that."

"Okay, but when I do, we're making a list of questions for my parents. They will explain this."

I stood with my back to the door, staring at Hal, my chin practically on the floor. I'd never seen him angry, nor even imagined it. And yet there he was, totally justified in it.

You've dropped the ball, Aliyah.

The evil inside voice sounded like it clicked its tongue even though it didn't have one.

The door hit me in the back as someone pushed through it. I tried leaning backward, keeping it closed, protecting my friends, but it was no use. My knees got weaker than a little door pushing should have made them. My head lighter too, so I knew who was trying to bust in.

"Get out of here, Alex." I turned, trying to push with my arms and get it to close, but his foot and his arm were already in the door.

"Why are you in there with the headmaster's son?"

"None of your business." I glared at him. "Shut off your poison immediately." He knew Hal was sick, and that room was small. "Or I swear—"

"Fire is a bad idea in there without the vent on, Aliyah." His chuckle was low and rolling. And entirely inappropriate in this situation. "So is poison. Which is the worse way to go, I wonder?"

Some folks would have been startled by a callous remark like that. Not me. Remember my first day? Yeah. Let's just say I wasn't reacting with a flight response here.

"I'm going outside, you guys."

I opened the door just wide enough to get out, physically blocking Alex from entering the room and pushing him out of the way. Even through the poison-induced haze, somehow, I found the strength. When Ember dropped down from the perch outside and above the sauna door, I understood.

My familiar channeled some of her strength into me. This was like that first day in the cafeteria, except I hadn't conjured any fire in my hands. It was all in my body, fighting the poison. I felt it burning out of me instead of through my veins, Ember helping me to use it as a purifying force.

"You are the pushiest person I know." I crossed my arms over my chest, blocking the doorknob with my body. "I can't believe you tried gassing a room with three people inside and then laughed about it."

"I'm shocked." He blinked. "I thought you'd have a sense of humor like my cousin. And ambition, like your uncle."

"Not really." I shook my head, finally getting the picture.

The evil inside voice had been right. Alex Onassis did admire me for being an extramagus. For all the wrong reasons. He was a bully but stuck with a subtle sort of magic, so he was looking for a partner with power, and he thought he'd found one.

But you're too kind. Such a shame.

"Not really," I repeated. "We're breaking up, Alex."

"That's sudden." He licked his lips. "Are you sure?"

"I should've talked to Noah sooner, and then it really would've been sudden." I snorted.

"Are you worried I'll cheat on you?" He rolled his eyes. "It won't happen again. If I'd known how powerful you were, I'd have kept my hormones in check around your brother's boy-toy."

"You never asked if I wanted to date you. You just assumed and followed me everywhere. Toxic City."

"Women want a man who takes what he wants." His chin was clenched, but his eyes darted from one side to the other. "I'll ask again. Are you sure we're breaking up?"

"You broke my brother's heart for kicks." I narrowed my eyes. "So yes, I'm sure."

"Aliyah, do you need help?" It was Faith. Her hands were shrouded in the faint gray of undeath energy, and she wasn't alone, either. Seth stood with all four of his feet planted on the tile, growling at Alex.

"Thanks for the back-up." I jerked my chin at Alex. "Maybe now he'll take no for an answer."

"Dumping me right before the game? That's classy." Alex smirked. "You're judging me for what happened on the first day. Honestly, I expected greater things from you."

"It's not something that happened; you made a choice." I shot a glance at Faith. "You knew Darren was Noah's boyfriend. You should have apologized and owned up. But instead, you act like you're too good for that."

"Wait." Faith blinked. "That was you? Jerk."

"I went to a great deal of trouble to keep my name out of that particular rumor mill." Alex looked down his nose at me. Or tried to, because we were almost the same height. "If it finds its way back in, be assured yours will join it."

"Wow." Dylan came around the corner, eyes in a constant state of motion between me, Faith, and Alex. "Did I just hear you threaten my friend?"

"Grow up, Khan. It's only quid pro quo." Alex dropped his hands to his sides. "If she doesn't want any trouble, my ex will fall in line. We'd better start warming up, getting prepared to play rough."

He walked away, but overall, I figured this was a victory despite his veiled threats. Sure, I ran the risk of having my secret outed before I was ready. Once I did, Alex Onassis and his rumor mill would have no power over me. I hoped.

"Is Hal in there?" Faith jerked her thumb at the sauna door.

"Yes, Grace too." I heard footsteps in the room behind me. "And they're done." I stepped aside and let my friend through.

Grace came out with my knapsack, packed up again. She handed it off, then headed toward the lockers, Dylan following. Faith went in to sit with Hal. When I peeked through the window, I saw them holding hands with their eyes closed, the paper with Bubbe's instructions on it beside them. They were doing the therapy, which involved using undeath magic to stabilize Hal's regulation of his space magic.

I stayed outside the sauna, guarding the door because the last thing I wanted was Alex learning even more secrets. He might know mine, having guessed correctly because he'd seen it before, but my friends shouldn't pay for my mistake in trusting him.

In about five minutes, the pair emerged, faces flushed and holding hands. The bond I always sensed between them was stronger than ever.

I walked with them to the lockers where we stored our stuff and changed. After that, we put on and tested our ankyr and cestus, including the new professional-grade ballistae. These were worn in televised tournaments. They added refinement to channeling so extra energy didn't escape our hands, making the conjure more efficient and less draining.

I realized that these ballistae might help the other types of extrahumans playing this sport. Part of the reason psychic energy and glamour were so hard to use for conjuring orbs was that they were more diffuse and harder to focus, but with gear like this that funneled as you channeled, maybe it was possible for them to really generate a good orb and throw it with accuracy.

Maybe that was how folks like Izzy could play. Precognition, telepathy, projection. Mentalist psychics, whose powers didn't otherwise manifest, now had a way to participate if they wanted to. Was this the big secret Izzy was keeping?

Coach Pickman blew her whistle. It was time for us to head out of the locker room and onto the court.

The first team we faced off against was my brother's. If it hadn't been for our conversation last week, this would have caused me no end of stress, but now there were no hard feelings, except the ones I carried inside, secret for now. I'd have to handle my confession delicately and do all I could to spare his feelings since my brother would always be important to me.

I stood behind Grace, waiting for Coach Pickman and the second-year team's Coach Ives to call for the coin toss. Noah caught my eye, nodding from his position as second defense. Our whole team already knew to watch out for his solar magic. He'd used it to blind other players before.

One reason this game was so exciting was that players could use tactics like that. As long as an orb was held in a defensive posture, moving around and letting its general effects just happen was perfectly within the rules.

Fortunately, we had Grace to counter that, and she excelled at staying on her toes. I fully expected this game to go long, potentially even for us to win since Hal's abilities were totally unknown to the other side.

The first defense guy was another air magus. They were pretty common, so it was no wonder the school had so many in attendance. He wouldn't be able to block my fire too well, so I could mostly ignore his defense and take him out as soon as I got the chance.

The other mid-players were both girls, earth and water, respectively. I wouldn't be able to do much against either of them, but Alex could negate both with relative ease. Considering his state of mind wasn't the best at the moment, I expected him to be especially fierce on the court. Hopefully, all the activity would take his anger down a notch or three.

Perhaps he could channel his anger at me into something constructive during this game. All the activity might even chill him out enough to reconsider the threatened vengeance angle. I might hope for the best, but I had no illusions about him apologizing anytime soon.

The person we really needed to worry about on the other team was their reverse point. It was Elanor Pierce, Logan's sister. I know, she didn't seem like the type to play competitive sports, let alone have any talent at it, but assumptions were bunk, so there you go.

She was uncommonly quick at conjuring her fire magic and throwing too. According to everything I'd read about her in the notes from last year, Elanor had also mastered the art of the fake-out. That meant she'd be able to conjure and misdirect almost everyone on our team. Part of team planning over the last month had involved me keeping an eye on her because I could sense fire energy. I'd be able to tell where she was actually aiming.

Other than that, most of what we'd do was protect Dylan. He had loads of stamina and could dodge most anything as long as we backed him up.

All we needed to do now was flip a coin.

CHAPTER FOURTEEN

The coin toss didn't go in our favor. I watched Noah conjure, calling forth his solar magic with a smirk on his face, which meant almost everyone on the team squinted or otherwise tried shielding their eyes.

He was my brother, so I knew better.

I stared him right in the eye, watching them widen as he realized I wasn't falling for his shtick. I conjured fire right back, and although I'm slower than him, it wasn't enough.

He wound up with both hands spinning his ball of daylight-bright solar energy. I knew he wasn't really going to blind my entire team, so I tossed my own orb in the air, knocking his out of the way before it could hit Hal in the chest. He'd covered his eyes and didn't see it coming, of course.

Maybe it would have been better for Hal, in the long run, to have let Noah's throw hit its mark, but there was nothing I could do about it now. Alex was there, leaping toward the middle to counter a chunk of earth heading straight for Dylan. It pattered to the ground, then vanished as the court's wards banished the energy. But Alex wasn't paying attention to his footwork, so he slipped on some before it dissipated and ended up on the floor.

This meant Dylan had no protection except his own air orb. I was still conjuring and didn't have enough to counter the ball of water coming straight for him, not that my element was much good against that anyway. But he had it handled.

Dylan's orb spun like a tornado, so when he held it up in front of his chest and pressed forward with it, the water orb appeared to shatter, bits scattering everywhere. Once the orb's cohesion broke, none of the droplets could tag us out. I got hit with a few, and they were almost impossibly cold. That was a helpful side effect of the unexpected shower. It stopped Hal from spacing out.

I wracked my brain, trying to remember any details about the alternative therapy Bubbe gave us, and there was one that might have accounted for that. The therapy was only possible because Faith used undeath energy, but that particular brand of magic came with its own set of problems when used on the living. Hal was a little bit zombified, which ended up being a good thing.

Elanor did one of her fake-outs. I sensed it, but she was so fast I didn't have time to warn my teammate. Hal didn't need one now that his eyes were open. Whatever Faith did, it gave him crazy reflexes. He blinked to one side as the fire orb sailed by, bouncing harmlessly out of bounds.

The girl casting earth stood there flabbergasted, leaving her wide open for Alex's orb. He hit her directly on the cestus, which flashed red as she was tagged out.

I hear Kitty, Eston, and Logan cheering from the bleachers. Our three friends were so gung-ho excited that we scored the first out, and that was where Dylan's gregarious nature failed him.

Dylan Khan was my favorite goofball in the world, so of course, he smiled and waved at our friends. It was a natural thing for him, but this game was unforgiving, so Elanor took her opportunity to throw another orb.

It must have been all the performance art training that had built her speed to that degree. I could imagine that in order to be entertaining with fire magic, you had to summon and banish your element with extreme alacrity. It served her well here, but her orbs ended up small and not so powerful. It was the same for Lee with his wood magic. I knew exactly how to deal with that.

By being stronger.

Grace had to hold her action in case Noah tried a blinding move, so I leaped into the middle, holding up my own fireball. Because it was the same element, Elanor's didn't dissipate. Instead, mine absorbed it, and I found myself breathless at how fast it all happened.

Or maybe it was the giant fiery orb eating all the oxygen next to my face.

My power level was exponentially larger than hers. She was a candle in the wind, while I was walking on the sun, but finesse could still win the day if I wasn't careful.

Throw it already before you incinerate yourself.

"Thanks, broken clock." I rolled my eyes along with the orb. Nobody needed to know I was talking to the evil inside voice, but I was. It was right.

I threw at Noah. He was the most dangerous player besides Elanor, who was better protected. The last thing we needed was someone getting blinded.

Ducking wouldn't help Noah, and he knew it. He hit the deck, flattening himself on the floor. He was as nimble as Grace. My fireball almost hit the mid-player behind him, but she managed to hop aside in time because I wasn't aiming for her.

I conjured again. It felt different. Why?

Solar magic. That's why.

"Stop. Banish time."

Beside me, Alex chuckled. I ignored him and conjured fire again, my focus intense. Meanwhile, Grace blocked a throw from their second defense. It would've hit me.

"Thanks."

She nodded and conjured shadows again.

Noah recovered with another sunlit orb, and everybody expected him to throw it instead of blinding us. But he aimed at Alex—at his head, not his cestus. I understood. He was angry. As much as I'd like to see Noah get revenge, I needed to make this play count.

So I launched my off-color orb. I missed, failing to deflect my brother's attack. Alex ducked, laughing. He avoided Noah's orb easily but took mine directly in the gut, sneering.

He wanted you to hit him, foolish girl.

His cestus flashed red, and just like that, Alex Onassis was out.

I blinked. How did this happen? The team's magic got calibrated to our equipment last week, so it shouldn't have triggered an out. But as my energy faded into Alex's protective gear, I saw it.

My orb had been solar magic after all, masked by a thin veneer of fire, which meant I had conjured both elements at the same time, using one to hide the other. And magicpsychic equipment doesn't lie.

A blast from Coach Chen's whistle cut the air, stopping the game.

I just told you there are no breaks in Bishop's Row, but that wasn't entirely true. If there was equipment failure or suspicion of cheating, any coach could call time out.

He led both teams to the sidelines where Coach Pickman, Headmaster Hawkins, and the second-year coaches waited. All four looked over Alex's equipment, checking for tampering or malfunction. They found nothing, of course, since this was all my fault.

They're going to catch you.

The singsong taunt from the evil inside voice was more than I could take. Yes, I was being a stereotypical fire magus and losing my temper. Anyone might have at that point. I'd spent months dealing with that incessant voice in silence. Not since the solar magic showed up. I understood now. It had first chimed in when I started lying. It was time to stop this insanity, or at least give it less to plague me with.

I raise my hand.

"Headmaster, I've got something to say."

"Step forward, Miss Morgenstern."

All my friends stared at me, mouths open and eyes wide. Except for Alex, who glared poison darts. Looked like I had made another enemy. I took a deep breath and prepared to own my mistake.

"I'm sorry, everyone. I didn't lie exactly, but I failed to report something. You have to disqualify me. Put Lee or Faith on the court in my place. This is my fault, not a malfunction."

"How?" The headmaster leaned forward.

"I thought I could control it just for one game. I was going to step down later. But now I have to say this in public."

"Say what, exactly?" Noah stepped forward. He was as pale as a vampire.

"Shh." Elanor put her hand on his arm, shaking her head.

"I'm an extramagus with solar magic." I raised my head, which felt weightless. "If that disqualifies me from Bishop's Row forever, I understand. If it's grounds for expulsion, I'll appeal through the proper channels with my parents."

"You're certainly not expelled, Miss Morgenstern." Headmaster Hawkins stood. "The athletic staff makes all the team decisions, including ability-related accommodations. However, I can't allow you to continue to play in this tournament."

"Somebody could've gotten hurt." Alex stepped forward. "If my equipment hadn't held up, I'd have second-degree burns by now."

"Not true." Coach Pickman snorted. "You were perfectly safe, Onassis. This court's got extra safety wards. I insisted after Morgenstern made the team. I hadn't forgotten the cafeteria incident that first day. Had you?"

"She lied. Won't she be punished?" Noah's question shocked me.

But it made sense. He was hurt again. I had blown my chance to tell him over break about all of this, and only a person completely bereft of empathy wouldn't realize Hal, Grace, and Dylan already knew my secret. My brother always caught the feels.

"Wouldn't you feel punished if you got disqualified for the whole tournament? They've been practicing for months." Coach Ives, the fellow in charge of Noah's team, punched his shoulder. "I believe that's sufficient. At least, I'm satisfied on behalf of my players."

"It's settled, then." Headmaster Hawkins nodded. "Coach Pickman will retrieve a new set of equipment for Mr. Onassis and choose a reserve player to replace Miss Morgenstern, who will accompany me to my office."

"Father." Hal tilted his head, wringing his hands. "Please stay."

"I don't know what this development's about, but I'll grant that request, Harold. However, Miss Morgenstern sits with me, not on the reserves bench."

"Thanks, Dad."

The headmaster led me to the sidelines, then toward a section of unoccupied bleachers. It was far away and not at the best angle, but at least we could watch the rest of the game. Probably, he wanted to make sure I didn't hurt anyone. Ironically, I felt like less of a risk to the people around me now than before my hasty confession.

Coach Pickman tapped Lee to take my place. I'd been hoping for Faith since she might have been able to help Hal if anything happened and he ran out of energy. I understood her strategy, though. With Elanor and Noah both capable of fast conjuring, she needed someone with speed. Faith was pretty fast, but nothing like Lee.

It was a jungle out there, in no small part because Alex was even angrier now. He played with a ferocity that could only come from extreme rage. I was worried about how the rest of the semester would go, sitting in classes with him.

I used to think he was neutral, like Switzerland, and this whole year, I had felt like the only person living a lie. I had been wrong. While my secret was a condition beyond my control, Alex took actions of his own volition. He hurt other people on purpose.

I knew there was a difference, but contemplating intent didn't make this easier. I had still lied, and people I loved were still in the dark. I sighed.

"How long have you known?" The headmaster kept his voice low even though the roaring crowd obfuscated it from eavesdroppers.

"Since the first lab." I hung my head.

"You're not the first extramagus on campus, you know."

"What?" I froze.

"Your grandmother had a brother. Same elements and everything."

"I've never—she's never spoken of him. Not once. There aren't even pictures."

"And you haven't told her." His voice was as deep and gentle as a cup of herbal tea. "Am I correct?"

"Yes." I nodded, wiping the tear off my cheek. Bubbe would have understood, after all. "Do you think she'll forgive me?"

"Peep?" Ember put her paws on my leg, peering at my lap, a signal she wanted to sit in it. I moved my arms to make room for her.

"There's only one way to find out. I want you to go home this evening after dinner. Talk to your family."

"Are you sending Noah home too?"

"That's up to him. But if he chooses to, I'll give you a head start. It's your responsibility to tell your parents, not his."

"Headmaster, th—"

My expression of gratitude was cut off by something horrible.

The whistle blew. Hal collapsed.

I didn't remember us rushing to his side, but that must have been what we did because we were there like no time had passed. Faith arrived first, then the headmaster. I stopped to stand with my friends, unsure what good my presence would do.

There was a tension in the gymnasium, one that could erupt into panic at any moment. I couldn't do anything to counter it because I might have been one of the sources. What was scarier than a magus collapsing due to an unknown malady? An extramagus standing up and taking initiative, of course.

So, I stayed back and left it to someone else to pick up the slack. And just like on Parents' Night, Logan Pierce stepped up and saved the day.

He dashed down off the bleachers, stacking equipment chests and standing on them so everyone could see him. After that, he opened his mouth and let out a cacophony of sound. I'd never seen anything like it, but somehow, I knew what Logan was doing.

He was talking to everyone's familiars like Doctor Freaking Doolittle.

Magi were subject to mob mentality like mundane folk or any

other extrahuman. A group of us incensed or frightened could cause serious harm, but when you added magical creatures into the mix, especially nervous ones with their emotions magnified in the echo chamber of bonds with magi, you had the potential for epic levels of disaster.

The noises Logan made were soothing somehow, despite their alien nature. He'd mastered practically every critter call in the book: peeps and chirps, warbles and coos, barks and growls, howls and meows, even whinnies and bleats.

The critters paused. One by one, I saw them relax. The airborne ones landed, and the landbound ones sat or laid down. Some cuddled together like the best of friends, while others ignored each other in comfortable silence.

The calm spread, overtaking the sea of troubled magi in moments. Each found his or her familiar nearby. It wasn't entirely silent in here since that was impossible in a gymnasium, but there was enough time and space for everyone helping Hal to do their jobs. For him to breathe.

Nurse Smith and Zeke lifted Hal on to a stretcher, an oxygen mask covering the lower half of his face. Seth jumped up on it, cuddling up with Nin. Faith kissed his forehead, then returned to the court and put on her equipment. She'd finish the game for him.

But the headmaster wasn't staying, not in the middle of his son's medical emergency, so neither could I. I followed him, joining the procession to the infirmary.

Once Hal was in bed with the transfusion tube in his arm, Headmaster Hawkins finally took me to his office. Instead of sitting at his desk, he stood with his back toward me, leaning on one of the built-in bookcases behind his seat as though he and the school held each other up.

I remained standing too, with Ember curled around my neck. It just felt wrong to sit when he hadn't yet. He was the ultimate figure of authority at Hawthorn Academy, but he was only extrahuman. This was his first year in this job, and his son was gravely ill, maybe dying.

He's weak. Use that. Prove your worth.

"No."

"Excuse me?"

"I said no, but not to you, sir." I walked toward the desk, then past it. Once I was beside him, I spoke again. "What I meant to say was, how can I help?"

"There's nothing you can do. Everything's complicated by my ex-wife. It's enough that you've befriended my son."

"Are you sure there's nothing I can do?" I turned my back and leaned against the bookcase, looking up at him. "My grandmother's got all kinds of medical connections. I can ask for her help."

"I know about the anonymous test." His Pharaoh's Rat peeked out of his blazer pocket, holding a yellow slip in his mouth. It had a serial number on it, the one from Hal's vial. I'd seen slips like this before. The courier service used them. "The diagnosis, too."

"Oh."

Headmaster Hawkins was a space magus. Their power went beyond just moving things around. I should have realized he'd know where his son was at all times and be able to track something as personal to him as a vial of blood.

Now he'll punish you. Perhaps even make you vanish forever.

He did nothing of the sort, of course. Most of the time, that evil inside voice was the biggest liar in the world. Thank goodness.

"Thank you. But that's about the extent of what your grandmother can do. The divorce designated my ex-wife to handle Harold's medical care. He's supposed to ask her."

I thought about my mother—the clipping she'd brought to Seder, and how it represented liberation from her toxic family. She'd called out a wrong when she had the chance. My friend needed some of that energy now, but his father had to know the truth.

"Hal says his mother's kept him from medical care even after he asked for it." I clenched my fists. "Isn't that abuse?"

"That's not how she tells it." He sighed.

"So, ask him." I closed my eyes, remember helping Grace. "Some-times the people who need help the most have the hardest time asking for it."

"I will." He cleared his throat, then turned to face me. "It's time you go home, Miss Morgenstern. I'll send a message ahead to your family. Professor Luciano will expect you in homeroom tomorrow morning."

"Thank you, Headmaster."

He clapped his hands, and just like that, I was on Essex Street outside one of the Ambersmith's shops with my knapsack dangling from my arm and Ember on my shoulder.

CHAPTER FIFTEEN

Our team lost. Faith managed to tag Noah out, though, and Dylan didn't go down until it was just him and Elanor Pierce left standing. They all got to show the school that first years weren't fooling around when it came to Bishop's Row.

I got grounded, of course. That was what happened when you lied to your parents for months on end, doing everything you could to cover things up. That meant I couldn't stay at school on the weekends since I was responsible for all sorts of chores around the house. Seriously big messy ones too—the spring-cleaning kind.

"You should have told us." Mom set a cardboard box beside me so I had somewhere to put all the dust bunnies. "I understand waiting the week out to be sure, but you came home the first weekend and told us all about that Charity girl and the fires. So, what happened?"

"It was because of that incident when we walked in, Mom. The Hopewell business." I leaned forward, reaching along the side of the dryer. This was the one in the basement that Bubbe used for all her medical linens, so it was extra dusty. "I didn't want you to start being afraid of me."

"I understand. But Aliyah, it's dangerous to go it alone as an extramagus." She sighed. "I suppose we could have done a better job of informing you and Noah, all things considered."

"Thanks, Mom."

"She's the one cleaning, and she thanks me." She smiled. "See? You're a good kid at heart."

"Less chatter, more dusting." Bubbe set a basket of dirty towels beside the washer.

My family still loved me. As far as the heavy chores went, I'd earned them, so while I didn't do all of the work with a smile, I completed every task using my best effort. Sometimes I fudged it a little, using my magic to help.

Bubbe wasn't ready to talk about her brother yet, except to tell me Dad had named Noah after him and that he'd died during the Boston Internment. That had me totally curious, but between working at home and all the homework from school, I was too tired to snoop around or do extra work to dig up info on the other Noah. She promised to give me the scoop this summer.

School wasn't much different on the punishment front. I was on honest-to-goodness detention, which wasn't anything like Familiar Bonding, unfortunately. Instead, I painted the bleachers in the gym and re-shelved books for the Ashfords in the library.

I had time for meals, class, and studying, and that was about it. The one silver lining was Alex couldn't mess with me. Kitty even kicked him out of her Truncheons and Flagons game. Neither could Charity Fairbanks. I noticed the two of them spending an awful lot of time together in corners around campus. Mostly, they whispered and pointed. At least she'd graduate and be gone next year, so I'd only have to deal with the poisonous magus.

But one thing happened that got me worried.

I was outside the lounge when I saw them, so I stepped back to the side of the doorway. It was shadowy, an ornately carved pillar framing it. Even so, I worried they'd see me until Grace joined me. With a wave of her hand, we were shrouded in shadows, courtesy of her umbral magic. Our concealment was so complete, Faith almost walked right into us. I dragged her into the occluding bubble, making a zipping gesture over my lips.

"I mean it, Charity." One corner of Alex's mouth tilted up, his eyes narrowing. "I'll do anything to show them we're better."

"Academic probation is no joke, kid." Charity was shorter and still managed to look down her nose at him. "You'll be on thin ice, just like Morgenstern, but for different reasons."

"I can handle that." He snorted. "I'll pass the classes easily."

"Okay, then." She unslung her oversized Hermes bag from her arm, setting it on the chair beside her. "Tempe's in charge, but you'll do the grunt work."

"And that'll let me get direct comeuppance?"

"On her and those pathetic sub-races she calls friends." Charity wrinkled her nose. "Ugh. I can't believe they'll be all over campus next year. But you and Tempe will do the right thing with the new crop of students. Add them to our cause."

"Will that be enough?" Alex chewed his lower lip. "Half of next year's graduating class doesn't understand that magi are meant to be the masters."

"You'll have no trouble if you play your cards right." Charity dropped him a wink. "They scare easily and freeze up. If you keep them out of it, the right side will win. That's why I'm entrusting you with this."

She opened her bag and removed one of those paper shopping bags, the kind with handles. It was shadowy, so we couldn't see what was inside. At least not until Grace pointed at it and called up more of her magic.

It was the Slayer's garb, the costume from the Night Creatures concert. Now that I saw it like this, I knew it was authentic. The Fairbanks were dyed-in-the-wool magisupremacists, extrahumans who'd hunted their own during the Reveal and even before it since magi can pass for mundanes.

Faith hung her head. Grace clenched her fists and ground her teeth. I stared, watching my evil ex-boyfriend reach into the bag and stroke the fabric with more affection than he'd ever shown his familiar.

"Oh, yeah." Alex hadn't smiled this much since the dance. "I'll rule the school next year."

"Tempe will." Charity's smile could have curdled milk. "You're behind her throne, not on it. Stick to our agreement, or I will break your name. You've got so many nasty little secrets."

"Understood." His grin was too broad, eyes too wide. She'd startled him.

"Have a great summer." She slung the large handbag over her shoulder and turned her back on him, tossing a tiny wave in his general direction.

Alex Onassis blinked after her for a moment. Once she was gone, he sank into the chair, rubbing his temples. I almost felt sorry for him, but almost didn't count.

"We need to tell the Headmaster." Faith's voice was hushed, which was good because even umbral shadows didn't hide raised voices. "If we go now, he'll catch Alex with that." She pointed at the bag by his feet.

"No, he won't." Grace shook her head. "We only see it because of my magic. That's a cloaking bag, magipsychic. He won't even know it's there."

"You can show him, though?" I waved my hand at the shadows above our heads. "Faith's right. Let's go."

"Good point." Grace nodded, directing us toward the wall so Alex wouldn't see us when she dropped the cloak.

But Headmaster Hawkins wasn't in his office. We didn't end up seeing him for the rest of the year. Professor Luciano said he was away from campus, dealing with a legal matter, and I couldn't be angry about that since maybe it had something to do with Hal's health.

Noah stopped talking to me again. It had me down, but not in a funk. Part of this was because it was my fault this time. There was no wondering why or second-guessing. Nobody to blame but myself. I had to atone, which meant both apologizing and trying to make it up to him. If I worked hard and showed him I cared, he might forgive me by the time Yom Kippur rolled around next fall.

Even with all the extra work and responsibility, I finally felt free. I might be days late to celebrate liberation, but at least I was nowhere near a buck short. None of my friends at school or at home were angry. Lee, Kitty, and Eston treated me the same as ever. I called a meeting in town to tell Azreal Ambersmith. Izzy and Cadence pretended this was the first they'd heard of it for his sake.

"I'm precognitive." Izzy rolled her eyes. "Saw something big coming, should have guessed."

"I didn't." Cadence elbowed Azreal, who was trying to steal some of her French fries. "But everyone in both worlds has secrets. I'd better learn how to handle that, especially if I want to be a good reporter someday."

"It's no big deal to me." Az shrugged, sticking to the food on his own plate. "Variety is the spice of life. Anyway, we've known each other practically forever. If magic starts giving you brain gremlins, we'll notice and help."

"I don't understand." I shook my head. "Being my friend could get super dangerous. I appreciate it and all, but I have to ask. Why put yourselves at risk?"

"Because you'd do it for any or all of us in a heartbeat, Aliyah." Cadence reached across the table, patting my hand.

"Yeah, and we're your friends." Izzy nodded. "We love you, Aliyah."

The detention was done, along with all the chores at home a week before final exams and the end of the semester. I spent most of my time studying in the lounge with Dylan, Grace, Hal, and Faith. And Logan, of course.

He didn't feel like a third wheel, but sometimes I did. It was hard to stop myself from laughing too loud at Dylan's jokes or watching him from across the room to half the time. But either I managed to keep it at a respectful level, or Grace knew and understood. Maybe a little of both.

I almost felt like my old self again, the Aliyah who'd walked along Essex Street with her family on the way to campus that first day.

Except I knew more about myself. I was still afraid of my strength, but not nearly as much because I had backup. That was more important than I could have imagined that first time through the migrating door.

We sat for exams, and this time, I wasn't the first person done. Alex stood up and stormed out of the room after only twenty minutes. We had three hours. None of us saw him study. There was no way he passed that exam without cheating. I wouldn't put it past him, but probably he didn't. Nobody looked that angry if they thought they'd passed a final in record time.

After lunch, there was no Lab, just another meeting in the home-room, where Professor Luciano posted our exam scores and then met with each of us for five minutes in private.

I was utterly shocked to find that Alex failed this exam, putting him below the GPA needed to pass first year. Everybody else scored above average or higher, with Hal at the top of our class. Logan surprised everyone by getting the next highest score. He was one point ahead of me, even.

Faith and I got the same grade, an A-. Bailey's was lowest but still in the B- range. She'd bombed two of the labs by refusing to work with Logan. When she complained, Faith told her to check her attitude and try teamwork next year. I was proud of her.

We were all moving up to second year except Alex, who was being held back. At least we could avoid him most of the time in second year, but Faith thought it was bad news.

"There's going to be trouble." She shook her head. "Temperance is coming."

"There's no throne for us to fight at Hawthorn Academy." Dylan snorted. "I don't see how this is a problem. With a name like Temperance, she can't be that bad, right?"

"Does Charity's name have anything to do with her personality?" Grace elbowed him in the ribs. "Except for being opposite, I mean."

"Grace is right." Faith sighed. "We have to watch out. Charity's been telling him about Tempe. They could team up, or worse, become a power couple. If that happens, we're screwed."

"It might be hard next year, but we can handle anything they throw at us." Hal smiled. "Because we'll do it together."

"We have to make through the summer first." Faith frowned, and I didn't blame her. She didn't want to go home, of course.

"I get it." Logan patted her on the shoulder. "Parents should have to take classes and get a license, like professional psychics and magi."

"I'm staying in town again." Dylan shrugged. "I've got a job at Walgreens this time. It pays way more than the Willows, and Brianna hooked me up. There are jobs all over town if you need one."

"I'm way ahead of you there." Grace leaned down, reaching to scratch Lune behind the years. "The Ambersmiths offered me some summer work, textiles stuff. I'll be super busy but in town."

"My parents won't let me stay." Logan shook his head. "Gotta keep learning the family business in what they call my spare time, but I'm going to insist they let me focus on critter calls instead of stunts and dancing."

"Good call." I grinned. "That's a handy skill to know. And more importantly, something you actually like. What about you, Faith?"

"My parents think it's pointless for me to spend even more time in Salem. The only way I can escape for the whole summer is by going abroad, visit the cousins in Geneva." Faith leaned against Hal's chair. "But I don't want to go that far away, not now. At least if I stay in New York, I can take the train up once in a while."

"Why aren't there summer classes or something?" I scratched my head. "That'd give you all the reason you need. Overachieving parents can't argue with trying to better yourself academically."

"There used to be." Hal reached up, taking Faith's hand. "But Dad hasn't got the faculty for that this year, or the time since he'll be with me down in Boston during the week for most of the summer. Dad sat me down with Mom and a lawyer, and she signed off on my medical care. I get to make my own decisions on it from now on."

Everyone smiled at that. It was about time Hal Hawkins, easily the most responsible of our entire group, had the chance to determine how he dealt with his illness.

"You guys, guess what?" It was Kitty. She dashed up to us, dragging Eston behind her as Lee followed along.

"What?" We sounded like a Greek chorus, answering in unison like that.

"It's about next year." She dropped Eston's hand and clapped hers. "It's finally happening. We're finally having intramurals! Can you believe it?"

"You mean we're competing against other schools?" I blinked. "But how?"

"In all the ways, of course." She grinned. "Show them the paper, Eston."

He smiled, cheeks flushing, and handed over the flyer. It had the names of three schools on it. Hawthorn Academy, of course, but also Gallows Hill and Messing Prep.

"This is going to be interesting." Lee nodded. "In all the ways, of course."

Lee Young couldn't see the future, but Izzy pretty much confirmed his sentiment when I visited her the day after school was over. We sat at Engine House with Cadence and Dylan, almost exactly like countless times last summer. Except Grace was there too now, and so was Lee. He got an internship at the museum.

"We'll all be visiting your campus several times next year." Izzy took a sip from her soda. "All the competitions will take place at Hawthorn because you guys are hosting."

"What are those again?" Cadence scratched her head. "The different categories, I mean. I can hardly keep track of them."

"Bishop's Row for one." Dylan chuckled. "And we'll win that one if I have anything to do with it."

"Oh, yeah, Mister Star Athlete." Grace waved her hand dismissively. "As if I won't be up there stopping orbs from hitting you. There's no I in team, you know."

"There's a crafting competition, too." Izzy chewed her lip. "But that'll probably be a tossup between Gallows Hill and us."

"Not if I have anything to do with it." Grace shook her head. "Ugh. Now I sound like Dylan."

We all laughed at that, Grace included.

"Isn't there something cooperative? You know, so we get to try working together?" Cadence batted her eyes at someone out the window. By the time I looked in that direction, whoever it was had passed by. But there was a jet-black tuft of down settling to the cobblestones outside.

"Yes." Lee nodded. "It's a collaborative lab. Students from each school team up to build magicpsychic devices, and they get judged by a panel of professors."

"What else?"

"A talent show." Cadence smiled, her teeth shining like pearls. "That one, I definitely remember."

It certainly seemed like next year would be complicated. That was probably an understatement. I thought we could handle it, though. Friendship had a way of making just about anything possible, and I had some of the best folks in the world on my side.

The End

Thanks for reading Aliyah's adventures during her first year at Hawthorn Academy! Don't worry, her story continues with *Light of Equality*.

Did you know there was another series set in the same world? Check out Providence Paranormal College to learn more about extrahumans on a whole different campus. You can find them, along with my other books, here: http://www.amazon.com/-/e/B00O6851HO

LIGHT OF EQUALITY

The story continues with book four, *Light of Equality*, coming soon to Amazon and Kindle Unlimited

GLOSSARY

People

- **Changeling**- A mortal child of either one or two faerie parents. Most changelings choose a monarch sometime in their twenties, although some do it earlier than they have to.
- **Dampyr**- The mortal offspring of two vampires. They aren't as rare as many suspect, although because their blood is exceptionally sustaining to vampires, they keep their status secret. Dampyr sometimes have magic or psychic powers that work unreliably.
- **Faerie**- A term used to describe either a changeling who has tithed to a monarch and spent a year and a day in the Under or the pure creatures such as Gnomes and Pixies who were created by the king and queen.
- **Ghost**- A dead person with unfinished business becomes a ghost. If a mortal makes a contract before death, that gives them unfinished business and lets them linger. When ghosts finish their business, they move on, but no one knows where they go from here.
- **Magus**- A mortal who can use magic. Magic comes from

energy in the world. Most magi can only use one type of magic. However, a rare few can do more than one kind. Those are called extramagi.

- **Merfolk**- People who can live on land with legs or in the sea with fins and tails. They only emerged from the ocean after the Big Reveal and are still extremely rare outside of harbor towns.
- **Psychic**- A mortal with psychic power. Psychic ability comes from a person's own body and mind.
- **Vampire**- An unliving person who drinks blood to survive and enhance their abilities. Only regular mortals, psychics, and magi can get turned into vampires. Shifters, changelings, and faeries won't turn, and most of those won't survive an attempt.
- **Shifter**- A mortal who can take an animal's shape. Shifters have one form, with coloring similar to what they have while human. They usually have an enhanced sense while human-shaped, which goes along with their animal. For example, an owl shifter might have keen eyesight and a wolf shifter, a great sense of smell.

Shifter Varieties

- **Dragon**- The only shifters who can see both magic and psychic abilities, though only while shifted. The most powerful ones can partially shapeshift. Dragons are immortal and reproduce infrequently. There are so few of them since the Reveal that they've started taking other magical shifters as mates.
- **Kelpie**- A magical shifter who gets their abilities from an enchanted faerie pelt that bonds with their soul. The Kelpie pelts were created by the Goblin King, so they have Unseelie energy and restrictions. A Kelpie's animal form is a horse. Families pass the pelts down through generations,

and part of each ancestor lives on to help their descendants. The ancestors can get distracting, however.

- **Selkie**- A magical shifter who gets their abilities from an enchanted faerie pelt that bonds with their soul. The Selkie pelts were created by the Sidhe queen, so they have Seelie energy and restrictions. A Selkie's animal form is a seal or sometimes a sea otter. They can use water magic as long as they wear the pelt. Families pass the pelts down through the generations, and part of each ancestor lives on to help their descendants. The ancestors can get distracting, however.
- **Tanuki**- A magical shifter with enhanced speed and the ability to see all types of magic while shifted. They are also the only creatures who can manipulate luck, causing it to turn from good to bad or the other way around. They stop aging if they own a charm infused with luck from humans. Very few of those charms exist, having been either used up during the Reveal or locked away.

Powers

- **Air magic**- The power to conjure, control, and banish wind or air.
- **Earth magic**- The power to conjure, control, and banish earth, sand, or rock.
- **Empathy**- A psychic power to sense and influence emotions in other people.
- **Fire magic**- The power to conjure, control, and banish flames.
- **Ice magic**- The power to conjure, control, and banish ice.
- **Lightning magic**- The power to conjure, control, and banish lightning.
- **Poison magic**- The power to conjure, control, and banish poison. Each magus has a slightly different type of toxin they produce. Some are even antidotes to others.
- **Precognitive**- A psychic power to foretell future events.

- **Spectral magic**- the power to conjure, control, and banish light.
- **Spectral Affinity**- A trait some spectral magi have that makes them charismatic and believable.
- **Summoner**- A psychic power that lets the user make contracts with pure faeries, letting the summoner call them in times of need. Each creature has an anchor, some item symbolizing the bond. Mastery of summoning takes decades of study, which is why the most powerful are either vampires or past middle age.
- **Seelie**- The Sidhe queen's court. The Seelie way is about following the letter of the law, even when it's hard or cruel. They have a hard time reconciling faerie rules with the new mortal laws since the Big Reveal.
- **Solar Magic**- The power to conjure, control, or banish sunlight. Some of the most powerful practitioners can find hidden objects or discover long-kept secrets.
- **Solar Affinity**- A trait some solar magi have that makes them beacons for coincidence.
- **Space magic**- The power to move the self or objects instantly across distances. Some can even move other people.
- **Space Affinity**- This space power comes with an ability to locate people or things important to the magus.
- **Telekinesis**- A psychic power that moves objects.
- **Telepathy**- A psychic power to read minds.
- **Tithe**- The process of pledging to either the queen or king, making a changeling choose to be either Seelie or Unseelie.
- **Umbral magic**- The power to conjure, control, and banish shadows and veil or camouflage objects or people.
- **Umbral Affinity**- A trait some umbral magi have that makes them difficult to remember without psychic ability, faerie magic, or a shifter pack bond.
- **Undeath magic**- The power to conjure, control, and banish unliving energy.

- **Unseelie**- The Goblin king's court. The Unseelies bend the rules and often navigate mortal society more easily than their Seelie counterparts.
- **Water magic**- The power to conjure, banish, and control water.
- **Wood magic**- The power to conjure, banish, and control wood. It takes extreme power to influencing a living plant.

Creatures

- **Basilisk**- A venomous serpent that also has poison magic.
- **Dragonet**- A tiny dragon-like creature, always associated with one or more element which powers their breath attacks later in life. They have scales but are warm-blooded like birds. Most don't get much bigger than a small cat.
- **Familiar**- A magical or mythical creature who makes a bond with a magus.
- **Gryphon**- A chimera which has the head of a bird and hindquarters of a predatory mammal. They come in several combinations of base species, and habitat influences their choice in magi to bond with.
- **Karkus**- A crab that can change its shape. They're said to be the offspring of the crab that pinched Hercules as he battled the Hydra.
- **Lightning Bird**- A familiar from South Africa with an affinity for lightning. Its beak can jump-start a car.
- **Mercat**- A shapeshifting feline with fur for land and scales in the water. They can live in lakes, rivers, or in the sea as well as on land. They must never completely dry out, or they will die.
- **Moon Hare**- A magical rabbit that gets power from its particular moon phase. They commonly bond with umbral magi.
- **Pharaoh's Rat**- These natural predators of dragon shifters are the size of ferrets and resemble a mongoose with more

fur. They have an affinity for space magic and can use it on occasion.

- **Pigeon**- Not as mundane as most think, some pigeons have an uncanny sense of direction due to their affinity for air magic.
- **Pricus**- An aquatic goat said to be descended from Capricorn. They can warp time even better than Gnomes.
- **Pure Faeries**- Creatures who spring to life from magical sources in the Under. They are genderless, and their type and ability depend on place of origin. They're associated with only one court, although they will work together to defeat a common enemy.
- **Sand Cat**- A feline that lives in the desert, able to go for weeks without water. Earth magic lets them do this.
- **Sha**- A magical desert dog from Egypt. Sha are the size of mundane toy breeds with short hair and small pointy ears. They could pass for mundane except for their blue tongues. They are attracted to anything undead.
- **Sphinx**- A magic cat with an affinity for fire. The reason they're hairless is that they're resistant to flames.
- **Strix**- A venomous owl with an affinity for poison. Female striges have rounded tufts on their heads, while males have pointed ones.
- **Sumxu**- A lop-eared cat found only in northern China. They are masters of camouflage and have an affinity for several kinds of magic.

Places

- **The Academy**—Something between a community college and a military academy for extrahumans, the Academy is geared toward helping extrahumans who don't play well with mortals get ready to join a blended society. It's got divisions for learners of all ages, though they are housed separately.

- **Cherry Blossom School**- A dojo geared toward teaching extrahumans self-restraint, meditation, and how to temper their enhanced physical abilities with more mundane skills. It's been around for close to a hundred years, run by the Ichiro family. Mundane classes used to be offered as a front but now are a separate division.
- **Ellicot City Magitechnic**- A prep school for magi and psychics specializing in magipsychic technology. It's located outside Baltimore.
- **Gallows Hill School**- Traditionally for shifters, this prep school in Salem recently opened its doors to changelings and other extrahumans not categorized as magi or psychics.
- **Hawthorn Academy**- A preparatory school for magi in Salem. Its campus is in the space between the mortal realm and the Under, giving it unrivaled privacy. They specialize in teaching familiar magic.
- **Providence Paranormal College**- A school founded just one year after Brown University and located right in its shadow. Providence Paranormal used to admit only magi and psychics, but it's been accepting all types of extrahumans ever since Henrietta Thurston became headmistress. There has been trouble since then for students and faculty, leading people to believe dissenters are sabotaging the school.
- **Trout Academy**- A prestigious preparatory school for changelings with magic, recently open to magi and magical shifters. Its campus is located in South County and has been operating in some form or another since Rhode Island Colony was founded.
- **The Under**- The faerie realm. It's been divided into two parts ever since the Sidhe Queen and the Goblin king split up thousands of years ago. Mortals don't age in the Under, but it's a dangerous place for them to be. Getting lost means never being seen again, and it's easy to get indebted to

something nasty while trying to get through or out of the Under.

- **Wolf Messing Prep**- An institute for psychics to learn to control their skills before heading to college.

Events

- **The Big Reveal**- The term used for the 1990s, when the world discovered magic was real and extrahumans existed. The decade was marked with fear as everyone adjusted to the changes. Since the 21st Century, law and technology work for both humans and extrahumans.
- **Boston Internment**- A reaction by Boston government officials to the disappearance and suspected trafficking in extrahumans, especially shifters. All registered extrahumans in Boston lived on barges for close to a month under guard by the Boston Police. The traffickers got their hands on some magical gadgets, rendering the protection useless. Few survived.

THANK YOU!

Thank you for reading! If you loved this book, please leave a review. You can find my other work by clicking the links below, going to **my website** or visiting my **Author Central page**.

ALSO BY D.R. PERRY

Providence Paranormal College

Bearly Awake (Book 1)

Fangs for the Memories (Book 2)

Of Wolf and Peace (Book 3)

Dragon My Heart Around (Book 4)

Djinn and Bear It (Book 5)

Roundtable Redcap (Book 6)

Better Off Undead (Book 7)

Ghost of a Chance (Book 8)

Nine Lives (Book 9)

Fan or Fan Knot (Book 10)

Hawthorn Academy

Familiar Strangers (Book 1)

Acting in Kindness (Book 2)

Fire of Justice (Book 3)

Gallows Hill Academy

Year One: Sorrow and Joy (Book one)

For other books by DR Perry please see her Amazon author page.

CONNECT WITH THE AUTHOR

Website: https://www.drperryauthor.com/

Join her newsletter!

Find more of D.R. Perry's books on Amazon.

OTHER LMBPN PUBLISHING BOOKS

To be notified of new releases and special promotions from LMBPN publishing, please join our email list:

http://lmbpn.com/email/

For a complete list of books published by LMBPN please visit the following pages:

https://lmbpn.com/books-by-lmbpn-publishing/

CPSIA information can be obtained
at www.ICGtesting.com
Printed in the USA
BVHW031347070721
611354BV00006B/83

9 781649 718655